Praise for]

"As the owner of a metaphysical shop, I cannot tell you how many times customers come to me with questions about improving their finances. Financial Sorcery has just made my life easier, as I can now point them to a book that has solid information about mundane and magical techniques that work. Jason Miller has collected wisdom from many sources, added his own spice, and come up with a pie you can sink your teeth into, rather the pie in the sky of other writings on money and magic. This book is real gold, not fool's gold, and I intend to make use of this treasure."

—Ivo Dominguez, Jr., author of Casting Sacred Space and Spirit Speak

"'Get rich quick' spell books are easy enough to find. Books that provide useful magical and mundane advice for improving your financial condition are far less common, and far, far more valuable when you find them. Jason Miller's Financial Sorcery is one of those books. If you read this book and follow Jason's advice, you will see real-time, real-world improvements in your financial condition and develop a new, healthier relationship with money. And I'm not just a reviewer, I'm a satisfied customer! Financial Sorcery provided me with many new strategies and ideas for improving my writing career. If you could use more money (and who can't?), you owe it to yourself to buy, read, and use Financial Sorcery."

—Kenaz Filan, author of The Haitian Vodou Handbook and Vodou Money Magic

"Jason Miller's Financial Sorcery is a tour de force of successful magical and life strategies to catapult the reader into a new and wealthy world. Although this book has more than enough spellwork ideas for the practitioner to achieve results, the real strength of the book is in teaching magical practitioners how to think about their relationship with magic, money, finances, and wealth in a way that grounds the magic into actionable steps. Although it would be impossible for any book to cover all the details, Financial Sorcery provides a rare glimpse into how to think about the process and movement toward wealth—an insight that is largely missing from most books on money or financial magic. I only wish I had written this book first!"

—Andrieh Vitimus, author of Hands-On Chaos Magic and host of "Deeper Down the Rabbit Hole"

FINANCIAL
SORCERY

FINANCIAL SORCERY

Magical Strategies to Create
Real and Lasting Wealth

Jason Miller
INOMINANDUM

This edition first published in 2012 by New Page Books, an imprint of
Red Wheel/Weiser, LLC
With offices at:
65 Parker Street, Suite 7
Newburyport, MA 01950
www.redwheelweiser.com
www.newpagebooks.com

ISBN: 978-1-60163-218-0
Library of Congress Cataloging-in-Publication Data

Miller, Jason, 1972-
  Financial sorcery : magical strategies to create real and lasting wealth / by Jason
Miller.
    p. cm.
  Includes index.
  ISBN 978-1-60163-218-0 -- ISBN 978-1-60163-597-6 (ebook) 1. Finance,
Personal--Miscellanea. 2. Magic. I. Title.
  BF1623.F55M55 2012
  133.4'3—dc23
                                                                    2012009711

Cover design by Ian Shimkoviak/*the* BookDesigners
Interior by Eileen Dow Munson

Printed in the United States of America
IBI
10 9   8 7 6 5 4 3 2 1

For my children, Matthew and Tegan.

ACKNOWLEDGMENTS

First and foremost, I wish to thank my wife and children for their patience and encouragement during the writing of this book. They were the inspiration for me to approach finances in a more serious way and thus are the real spark behind this book.

Special Thanks to Matthew Brownlee for more than 20 years of friendship, for helping reify the Lightning Glyphs of Jupiter, and for providing all the artwork for this book. Bang-up job, my friend.

Thanks also to Gordon White of Rune Soup for providing ideas, resources, and conversation. Thanks to Jow, Deborah Costellano, Rufus Opus, Michael Cecchetelli, and many others for reading parts of the first drafts and testing some of the magic therein.

Thanks to the Gentlemen for Jupiter, who serve as constant inspiration and companions in the effort to make necessary wealth a part of spiritual practice. Ave Iovis!

Thanks to all my initiators, mentors, teachers, friends, and informants who have revealed to me the secrets of their craft. Special thanks for this go to: John Myrdhin Reynolds, Namkhai Norbu, Lopon Tenzin Namdak, Kunzang Dorje Rinpoche, Cliff and Misha Pollick, catherine yronwode, Tau Nemesius, Paul Hume, Simon, Lama Wangdor, Blanch Krubner, Dr. Jim, and all my brothers in the Terra Sancta Sodality.

Lastly, I want to thank all at New Page Books who worked on this book. Specifically Laurie Kelly-Pye, who read an article of mine on Witchvox.com and suggested I start writing books.

CONTENTS

INTRODUCTION

C hances are good that if you have been practicing magic or witch-craft for any length of time, you have been asked a question that goes something like this: "If magic is real and you can cast spells, why aren't you rich?"

Most of us dismiss that question because if we are serious about magic, becoming rich is usually not our main concern in life. We have other motivation for what we do. If you think about it, though, the question actually has some validity. I mean, why not? Most of us work just like other people do, and need money just as everyone else does. When you take the snide skepticism away, we are left with a legiti-mate question: If magic is real, and spells work, why are we not more successful with money magic? When you take a look at the occult and pagan community, you can see it's not just a matter of being rich; many of us are not even financially stable. This is becoming more evident now that we have a generation of leaders and authors in the community who are at retirement age and older, and have to rely upon frequent calls for charity and assistance just to keep a roof over their heads, food on the table, and medicine in the cabinet.

I spent quite a lot of time thinking about this question of money and magic, and I started talking to others about their experiences. I came to the conclusion that the magic itself is fine: our spells usually work, the spirits bestow their gifts, and the gods respond when we call. The problem is in the application of our magic.

Almost everyone I spoke to about financial magic told me stories of how they used magic to fix a problem rather than build something for themselves. I was told stories of successful magic aimed at not getting fired, or obtaining emergency funds to pay bills. The attitude for most people seemed to be that when everything was okay, it was best to not give much thought to money at all. When people did talk about doing magic to attain something better for themselves, it was almost always for something pie-in-the-sky like the Mega Millions lottery. Though the aim of such a spell is to attain something greater than what you have, the real attitude behind it is still the desire to not have to think about money. Whether you are marginalizing the role it plays in your life by ignoring it or trying to get so much of it that you never need to think about it again, the goal is avoidance of money rather than engagement with it.

My own experience with money magic up until that point had mirrored that of my informants. Throughout my 20s and early 30s I had no interest in money outside of the bare minimum. I was what in the 1990s we liked to call a slacker. I used magic to address emergencies that arose in my hand-to-mouth lifestyle, and I did not think of anything else. In fact, I basically considered focusing on money to be un-spiritual. This is an attitude that was shared by many of my friends, and still is today by many people who practice magic and witchcraft.

Examining this brought me to an important realization about money and the spiritual path.

If you will grant me the indulgence to talk a little Bible, I'd like to share one particular verse that has had a profound influence on how we in the West view money and spirit. In the Book of Matthew, Christ says, "You cannot serve both God and Mammon," mammon being a word that means "money," but also implies a demon. Though I am writing a book on (financial) magic, this is a sentiment I tend to agree with. You cannot serve mammon and spirit. Those who serve money tend to become slaves to money, which tends to run counter to the aims of spirit. Money can corrupt those who serve it as surely as any demon can, and I think it is fair to say that a lot of the problems facing our world today are caused by people who are obsessed with money.

So how do you avoid serving money? One way that people avoid serving Mammon is by ignoring him entirely. This may in fact be the best way from a purely spiritual perspective. Certainly since the counter-culture hippie movement of the 1960s and 70s, anti-materialism has been commonplace among witches and magicians. It is a noble tactic and one that really works if you do it wholeheartedly. The problem is that most people do not do it wholeheartedly. If you are going to do it, then you really need to do it! There are only two ways this has been a successful approach: become a monk or nun, or become a homeless wanderer. Anything short of this is just kidding yourself. Thinking that merely working at a coffee shop and not wearing a suit is a non-materialist lifestyle is just the worst of both worlds.

For those wishing to become monks or nuns I have a list of contact info for Buddhist and Catholic monasteries you can apply to. If you would rather wander the earth I also have the number of Tom Brown Jr.'s Tracker School, which includes survival training, in the New Jersey Pine Barrens. Spend a few weeks with him and you'll be able to walk into the woods and be self-sufficient there for life, with just a good knife and the clothes on your back.

So are you ready to take the plunge into a real non-materialist spiritual path and give up your former life? No? Me neither.

For me this option of giving up the Western lifestyle was real. A Tibetan lama offered me the chance to stay in Nepal and study with him as a Yogi for years and years. When I said no (as I suspect he knew I would), I realized that if I was not going to take a non-materialist path in a serious way, I would need to bring materialism onto the spiritual path in a serious way.

If we cannot serve money, and we cannot avoid money, that really leaves only one option: to master it.

Magical people—pagans, witches, mages, sorcerers, and so on—are ideally suited to accomplishing this goal. We have experience in taking things the rest of society has deemed sinful and making them sacred:

- x We have taken sex and made it a healthy part of the spiritual path.
- x We have taken radical freedom of expression—the right to be gay, kinky, and straight up freaky—and made it part of the spiritual path.
- x We have taken spells and magic and made them part of the spiritual path.

It is for this reason that the very people who will read this book are in the ideal position to take financial wisdom and join it with spiritual wisdom. To marry fiscal responsibility to environmental responsibility and make the financial craft a part of the witch's craft. To take the magical arts and apply them to the fiscal arts.

A Few Things to Keep in Mind While Reading This Book

First and foremost, I am not a financial services professional. I do not have a degree in economics or any related field. The non-magical advice in this book is fairly mainstream and common-sense, but should not be considered the advice of a professional.

Second, much of the information in this book is based on the economy, businesses, and laws of the United States. Most of the information in the book will be applicable to people in other countries, but some of it may not be.

Last, please keep in mind that magic is an art that can have drastic effects on one's life and psyche. Even seemingly simple practices such as meditation can bring up repressed thoughts and memories. Contact with spirits and gods can at times be jarring and open up unwanted communications. Spells may manifest in ways that you do not expect or plan for. If you have no basic training in the magical arts, you may want to first seek out such training from another individual, group, or book (see the resources at the end of Chapter 3).

Chapter 1

PERSPECTIVE

Before you can plot a course, you need to know a few things. You need to know your current location, the lay of the land that you are going to traverse, the methods by which you will make the journey, and, most importantly, at what destination you want to arrive and why you want to arrive there. This will give you proper perspective for your journey.

The path to a financial goal is no different. This chapter is all about gaining perspective:

- x Perspective on where you are financially right now
- x Perspective on the financial environment you live in, and the opportunities and obstacles it presents
- x Perspective on what magic can actually accomplish and how best to apply it

Your Personal Situation

The first thing most people think about in conjunction with wealth magic is the desire to be "rich." Most people don't have a clear idea of what this means, and those who do typically tell me that what they want is to have enough money that they never have to think about it again. I know a few people who are what many people would call rich, and I can tell you that all of them think about money. A lot.

As I pointed out in The Sorcerer's Secrets, terms such as rich and wealthy are relatively meaningless. The truth is that on a global scale, almost everyone who is reading this book is rich. According to the World Bank Development Research Group, anyone making more than $47,500 a year is in the top 1 percent of income earners on planet earth. If you make more than $25,500 a year, you are in the top 10 percent of income earners. The bottom 50 percent of the people on planet Earth live on less than $800 a year. Think about that for a moment.

I know you're thinking that $25,000 may be in the top 10 in the world but it's still pretty poor for America, where the federal poverty line is currently listed as $10,787 for an individual. But let me remind you that even the poorest people in America or Western Europe have access to amenities that the poor in most of the world do not. The roads, sanitation systems, plumbing, and access to charitable services and social safety nets are things that the bottom 50 percent will never see. The simple idea of potable water coming out of a faucet is a foreign idea to much of the planet. The guy flipping burgers at your local diner may live close to the poverty line in America, but that still puts him among the top 10 percent wealthiest people on the planet, and his life reflects that.

Am I saying that you should just be happy with what you have and not strive for greater wealth? No, most definitely not! I am all for you attaining greater and greater levels of wealth. If your desire is to be rich enough to own your own jet, then I say go for it! My point is simply this: You can't do magic with merely the aim of being rich. If you summon Jupiter and ask him to make you wealthy, he is going to look at you funny and remind you that you are probably already in the top 10 percent, if not the top 1 percent. If, however you ask him to help you reach specific goals, and you present him with a detailed plan, he is probably going to be a lot more helpful. You need perspective about where you are and where you want to be, as well as a plan to get from here to there.

Being Rich vs. Being Wealthy

Being rich and being wealthy are not the same thing. A rich person has a high income, which is a stream that can feed being wealthy or being in debt, depending on how that money is used. There is no shortage of people with high incomes but no real wealth. Do you think Canadian singer-songwriter Leonard Cohen wants to be on tour at age 76? Of course not. Do you think famous photographer Annie Leibovitz wanted to put the rights to her photos up as collateral for a loan? Absolutely not. One needs only watch a show like VH1's Behind the Music to see a long line of rich people whose income was used to build debt rather than wealth.

Wealth is not a flow of income; it is a state of positive finances. Buckminster Fuller once said that wealth can be measured in the number of days that one can live one's normal lifestyle without a paycheck. When your assets and sources of passive income are high enough to provide sufficient income to support your lifestyle without your having to work for a paycheck, you are wealthy. I like this system of measurement.

Note the relationship between lifestyle and income. If you are happy in an apartment or small house in a rural area, the income needed to create wealth is less than if you owned a brownstone in Manhattan. It places the ball squarely in your court to figure out what you want and what you need to do to achieve it.

Using this measurement you can begin to chart where you are in terms of income, expenses, and debt, and where you need to be.

The specifics of doing this are what the rest of the book is about. Before we get to that, though, we need to look outward. It is not enough to know your own financial situation; you need to know the financial situation of the world.

The World's Financial Situation

I am writing this book in the final months of 2011, and at the moment the financial situation is pretty bleak. America has been experiencing the worst economy since the Great Depression, and it has been that way since early 2008. Unemployment has been hovering around 9 percent for four years straight and shows no signs of improving. More than a quarter of America's homeowners are upside down on their mortgages. Even government-run parks and libraries are closing their doors. Europe is now entering a crisis even worse than what America is going through, and entire countries are in danger of defaulting on their loans. Bonds, once thought to be the very safest of investments, are reaching record lows.

The gap between rich and poor is growing daily, and the system is increasingly stacked to reinforce the divide. According to Mother Jones magazine, the top 1 percent of Americans control 34.6 percent of the nation's wealth. The rest of the top 10 percent have another 38.5 percent of the nation's wealth, which leaves the bottom 90 percent with only 26.9 percent of the nation's wealth. This type of income inequality normally only exists in third-world countries. This divide has sparked the "Occupy Wall Street" protest movement, which has now grown in size, public profile, and importance to a degree that is unmatched by any protest movement since the 1960s.

More and more people are finding it difficult to manage in the current economic environment. In fact, most people have difficulty even understanding it. Unfortunately, knowledge about how finances work is not often taught in schools. It should be, but it isn't.

The Deal

Instead of financial education, society offers us a deal: It provides us enough education to be mediocre and not make too much of a fuss, to get a good job with good security, to show up on time, and to clock in and out until we are 65. In exchange we get enough money to make us comfortable enough that we won't start asking too many questions or do a re-run of the French Revolution.

The problem is that the deal we were educated for is no longer the deal. That was the deal our grandparents got.

Here is the new deal:

No job security—Apart from the 10-percent unemployment rate, the employment offering rate is so low that even if every job in America were filled tomorrow, 5 out of 6 people on unemployment would still not have jobs.

No raise—Chances are that the job you had and got laid off from will either not be there or will be paying half of what you were making before. If you managed to avoid a layoff, you might have had to take a pay cut. With an average of 400 people applying to every professional position, employers can pay bottom-dollar wages.

No retirement—Unless you work for the government or a university, pensions have been gone for a long time, and 401k matching contributions are going away, if they are not gone already. Even some government pensions are disappearing, and some people who are already retired are seeing the pensions they were promised being cut drastically. According to the Transamerica Center for Retirement Studies, 70 percent of workers report that even if they work full time until age 65, they will not have enough money to retire.

This is the new economy and it is the result of what happens when money becomes the master of its handlers rather than the other way around. It is what happens when spiritual worth is divorced from material wealth.

That's the bad news. Here is the good news: Times of upheaval are also times of unprecedented opportunity for building prosperity by throwing off the old deal and making our own. You need the willingness and daring to stop acting like unthinking cogs in a machine and start re-engaging your genius and creativity to do something radical.

The Internet has made it easier than ever to start a new business with very little money invested, allowing you to test your ideas with very little risk and overhead. As American and European markets struggle, emerging markets are popping up strong and are open to foreign business. For every business model that is dying off, there is at least one more taking its place. You just have to be willing to change along with an ever-accelerating world.

To use a business cliché, it takes thinking outside the box, and there is one thing that I know for sure: Pagans, witches, magicians, and sorcerers know how to think outside the box! We have creativity and genius and strength of spirit. There is no longer a well-trod path for living a prosperous and happy life. Today we must make our own path, and magical people are good at that.

What Financial Magic Can and Can't Do for You

I know that magic works. If you are reading this, you probably also know that magic works. You can do a spell and, depending on various factors, there is a high probability that it will manifest a result. This book arose from my repeatedly asking this question: "If magic works, why aren't more of us better with money?" The answer that I have found is that although magic works, we often do not apply it in the most strategic manner. Individual spells may work for drawing money, but often these are not done within the overall context of a financial strategy, and thus do not lead to real wealth. Moreover, many people have incorrect ideas of what magic can do and how to link magical and mundane action. Most of this book is about how financial magic works and what it can do for you. First, however, we need to talk about what I consider to be the most common mistakes in financial magic, and also dispel some myths on the topic. Let's start with the idea of emergency magic.

Emergency Magic

Emergency magic is bad magic. I cannot tell you how many people tell me that magic should only be used to fix problems that cannot be fixed through mundane means, and even then only as a last resort. There are three main problems with this line of thinking.

The first problem is that it treats magic as something fundamentally different from any other type of action—something that works outside the forces of nature. Magic is not like that. Magic works within nature, is part of nature, and is subject to the same ethics and considerations as any other type of action.

The second problem is that by treating magic as something only to be used as a last resort, you are almost guaranteeing that you will not be very skilled in the use of magic. Think about it. How do you get good at something? Practice. If you never use magic, what makes you think you will be adept enough to deploy it when you need it?

The third and most important consideration is that by the time a situation is an emergency, it is usually also too late to do much with magic. The few times I have been called upon to do magic to save a dying business, the situation was so dire and the debt so high that all I was able to do with magic was supply an exit that left my clients in as little debt as possible. Had magic been used all along, from the start, things might have been different. Strategic sorcery is done ahead of time and according to a plan so that those problems don't occur, or at least get fixed before they get out of hand.

Reactive Magic

It has been my experience that about two thirds of what people use money magic for is not growing wealth, but maintaining the status quo. Although this type of magic does have a place, it can also be dangerous if you do not approach it with wisdom. Not dangerous in the sense of backfired spells or summoning demons, but dangerous in that it is much too easy to stay trapped in a crappy job or living situation by fixing all the issues that might otherwise force you to do better for yourself.

Sometimes what seems like an emergency is actually the universe opening up an opportunity that you could then take advantage of with your magic. Certainly, just as with emergency magic, you will occasionally need to use magic to maintain a situation that you like and that is good for you. The trick is distinguishing a truly good situation from a merely comfortable one. Comfort can be the enemy of growth. When using magic, make sure you are growing and not stagnating.

The Lottery

The last thing I want to talk about is the lottery. In my Strategic Sorcery Course the first homework assignment is to set a strategic goal to attain using a combination of magical and mundane methods. Two of the first 10 people who sent in their homework answered that they wanted to win millions in the lottery. This was a terrible disappointment as it is not where people should be focusing money magic.

Apart from spiritual growth and enlightenment, practical magic can do two things: it can affect the minds of other people; and it can shift probability in your favor, making improbable things more probable. Some things, however, are so improbable that even major magic will not be sufficient to manage it—the big pots in the lottery are like this.

Just to give you an idea, although it varies by state, on average, your chance of winning the big pot in a lottery is 1 in 18,000,000.

Your chance of being struck by lightning is 1 in 2,650,000—about 45 times more likely than winning the lottery. If you drive 10 miles to buy a lottery ticket, you are 30 times more likely to die in a car accident on the way than win the lottery!

I know it seems as though winning the lottery is not that improbable; almost every week someone is on the news talking about what they will do with their winnings. The thing is that if they ran one-minute interviews of everyone who lost every week, they would need two entire channels running nothing but those interviews 24 hours a day.

Doesn't magic increase your chances, though? Of course it does—as it does for everyone else using magic to win the lottery. Perhaps it reduces your chance from 1 in 18 million to 1 in 9 million or even 1 in 1 million. Still not great odds.

Because two out of the first 10 people who gave me their goals wanted to win the lottery, it's pretty safe to assume that there are thousands of people aiming their magic at any given lottery pot. Everything from complex rituals to seven-day candles to novenas are being used, all the time. Most of this magic cancels the other magic out and more or less evens the odds again.

Now here is the best part. Let's say that through super-powerful magic and sheer chance you manage to win! According to wealth counselor Szifra Birke, about one-third of lottery winners find themselves in serious financial trouble or in bankruptcy within just five years of winning.[1] This is because they never took the time to understand money or how it works. If they did, they wouldn't have pinned their hopes and dreams on willing the lottery.

That said, I usually buy two tickets for each one: one, because you have to be in the game to win it at all, and a dollar is certainly worth that; and two, because it also seems worth another dollar to double my chances. After that it is diminishing returns, and I do not devote any more money, and certainly no more time, to the lottery. I am not against playing the lottery; I am against incorporating it into your financial strategy for your life.

The same goes for other types of gambling, by the way. If you know enough about games of chance that you can gamble professionally, then certainly magic can help you, but at that point you are not really gambling—there are other skills that go into it.

Once we know where we are with our finances and what magic can and can't do for us, we're ready to focus on getting perspective on money itself—not only as a material force, but also as a spiritual one.

Chapter 2

MONEY AS SPIRIT

As I mentioned previouly, in the gospels of Mark and Luke, Christ refers to money as a spirit named Mammon. The word mammon is still in use today as a term for money in Finnish, Hebrew, Dutch, Czech, and German. The characterization of money as a spiritual entity is a good one, and an important one for sorcerers to understand. Though I do not believe that money is a literal spirit, it does share many of the characteristics of a spirit, as surely as a demon in a medieval grimoire does.

Money, like a spirit, is intangible and invisible. The cash and symbols that represent money are similar to sigils and talismans. Despite its intangible nature, money can create very concrete effects in people's lives by its presence or absence. More importantly, money requires certain offerings and has certain protocols for handling it if you want it to remain friendly. If money is mistreated, it will leave as surely as an offended guest. If you become too invested in it, it can possess you as though you were Linda Blair.[1]

Whether money acts as an angelic or demonic spirit largely depends on how you handle it. This is where Christ's advice about Mammon comes in: "You cannot serve both God and Mammon." This doesn't mean that money is in and of itself evil, but that you cannot serve money. It must serve you. This is no different from the ceremonial magician's evocation of demons. When evoking a demon, you bind it to oaths and make it submit to your will, which is aligned to the divine will. It must serve you, not the other way around. You are in fact fulfilling the natural order of the universe by commanding the demon in the name of divine will, and thus exposing it to the divine light. Money is no different: tame it and make it serve you or you will end up its servant—or worse, its victim.

As an example, I know a hedge fund manager who is quite rich. However, I would not call him wealthy because he is a slave to his money. Working 80 or 90 hours a week will make you a lot of money in the right profession, but working so much that you have no time to enjoy your money, outside of drinking yourself into oblivion every weekend, is not what I would call wealth. This person is not mastering money; money is mastering him.

On the other end of the spectrum is a friend who is not able to handle money at all. He doesn't know how to get it, and even when he gets some, he can't hang on to it. No matter how much he makes, he always seems to live hand to mouth. Different dynamic, but also a case in which money is the master.

It's important that you develop a healthy and balanced relationship with money. Many people involved in spiritual paths tend to be so anti-materialist that they develop unhealthy relationships with money. If you really want to walk the anti-materialist path there is nothing wrong with that, but as I mentioned already, really doing it requires being a monk or a nun or a homeless wanderer. Working a

40-hour-a-week job that you claim not to care about does not constitute a non-materialist path.

If you cannot serve money, and you do not wish to avoid money, the only alternative is to master money. If you want money to work for you, you need to learn about it, just as you would a spirit. Spirits have very specific likes and dislikes, and so does money. Certain protocols and attitudes attract certain spirits, and it is the same with money. Here, then, are the various qualities of the "spirit" of money.

Honor

Money likes to be valued. It likes to be liked. On the surface this sounds silly; I mean, who doesn't like money? When you get past that surface reaction, though, a lot of people realize that they do not actually value money; rather, they have a distrust of those who have money, and generally see money as a necessary evil rather than a potential force for good.

When people think about love and relationships, it is common to hear, "I don't care how much money he or she makes"—yet the number-one cause of divorce is money troubles. We have already discussed how, when people get involved in magic or spirituality, there is a tendency to see money as material and unspiritual—yet one of the biggest problems that magical and pagan groups encounter is funding the projects they have. Those who dedicate all their time to being leaders and teachers in pagan and magical communities, without giving much consideration to money, are often rewarded with poverty in their golden years.

The distrust of money is especially prevalent in young adults. Certainly, when I was in my 20s, I mistrusted money and thought the problems of the world were caused by those who possessed money. The Occupy Wall Street protests are a great if exaggerated example of this mindset. I am sure that you have seen the "I am one of the 99 percent" slogan—meaning the 99 percent that controls less of the country's wealth than the remaining 1 percent of the super rich. Looking around at the problems of the world it is easy to see why people would distrust or even hate money.

The difficulty is that most problems require money to fix. And for every affluent person screwing up the world, there is another quietly donating millions to charity. Sometimes it's the same person! Money is not the problem; people are the problem. Solutions to the world's problems will not be thought of by people who hate money, nor will they be thought of by people who are dominated by money: They will be thought of by people who honor money and its role in the world. They will be enacted by people who have the money to make them work.

You can protest until you are blue in the face that corporations should not be greedy, but it will do no good. Corporations exist to make money, and if they are public, they are accountable to their shareholders; it is literally illegal for them not move in ways that make profit for the shareholders. However, if people work to make doing the right thing profitable, corporations and affluent people will follow.

So, if you want to improve your finances, it is important to like money. You don't need to obsess over it or make it the center of your life. You need to like it enough to learn about it. Like it enough to honor its place in your life and in the world.

Movement

Many people think of money as a stationary thing that one possesses; like the coins in Scrooge McDuck's vault, it is just sort of there in a big pile. But the truth is that money likes to move. Money never stays still. You are always either making money or losing money. This is the root of the old cliché that you have to spend money to make money. Money circulates. It is traded for goods and services, exchanged in markets, gambled in casinos or derivatives markets, entrusted to banks to invest for you, and is generally in a constant state of motion.

If you are the type of person who stuffs money into the mattress, it is time to get it in motion.

What this means for the sorcerer is that rather than doing simple spells for drawing in sums of money, the focus should be on managing the flow of money through your life. Everyone has a pile of money coming in and a pile of money going out. If the pile coming in is bigger than the pile going out you will build wealth. If the pile of money going out is bigger than the pile of money coming in you will build debt. It's that simple. The amount of money in the piles has almost nothing to do with the process. There are people who make six or seven figures and can't make ends meet, and people near the poverty line who manage to save a tidy bundle for retirement.

Some people are cunning enough to make money simply by moving it around or betting on how it will move around. Forex traders, derivative investors, day traders, and the like produce nothing; they simply bet on the motion of money. That is not something that can be taught in a book like this, but it is done every day. I know of one coven of witches whose primary work outside of honoring the god and goddess is using divination on the stock market. So far they have done quite well for themselves.

Waste

Part of honoring money is not wasting it. We all have different ideas about how money should be spent. What might seem like a waste to one person is a great pleasure to another. For the purposes of this book what I am calling waste is spending that causes debt or takes away from important things and that does not bring very much enjoyment considering the cost.

When I give classes on financial sorcery I often ask how many people know someone who is perpetually in debt and has trouble making ends meet. Everyone knows someone like this. I then ask how many of those people have enormous DVD collections. There are always a lot of chuckles from the crowd because, again, most people know someone like that. They can't pay their rent, but they buy every DVD they think they might ever want to see, even though they will probably only watch it once, if at all. Worse yet, they usually buy it the day it is released for twice as much as it will cost two months later. This is money that should be spent elsewhere and that doesn't bring much enjoyment. This is a waste.

If the same DVD collection existed in the house of someone who had no trouble making ends meet, had a solid financial life plan, and was generally comfortable, the money spent on it is not a waste. It may not bring a lot of enjoyment either, but it's not pure waste.

In everyone's life there are some things that you just get too much enjoyment out of to cut, even if you are in debt. My sin is Starbucks. Even when I could be putting those three bucks toward something else, I just enjoy it so much that I get my Americano anyway. There are some financial writers whose message seems to be nothing but austerity and cutting expenses—this is not my view. Life is for living, and cutting out all of life's small enjoyments is no way to get ahead.

Gambling is another prime example of how people can waste money. I am not talking about those who can afford to blow some money on games of chance once in a while. I am talking about those who have a compulsion, or who honestly think that it is the path to wealth. At least a few times a year people write me wanting to purchase a gambling charm because they need to win enough to feed their family or pay their bills. They never write back when I tell them the first thing they need to do is stop gambling.

Most of us know when we spend money we shouldn't. We usually do it more out of habit than out of genuine enjoyment. Identify where you waste money and cut it out. (More on this in a later chapter.)

Charity

Do you know someone who tithes to his or her church? A tithe is a gift of 10 percent of your income to your church or spiritual institution. Far from a hardship, everyone I know who does this reports back that they experience a financial benefit from the giving in the form of opened opportunities and increased flow of money into their lives.

Money likes to be given away. It likes to be donated. If you understand money's mobility, you will understand that giving money will open up an opportunity for the universe to give back. It is said that gripping money too tightly will mean that your hand will never be open enough to receive.

Eleanor Roosevelt once said, "When you cease to make a contribution, you begin to die." Almost all wealthy people give a significant amount of money to charity. They do not do it just because society expects them to; they do it because they understand the nature of money and because it is part of what makes their own lives worthwhile.

The power of giving in relation to creating wealth is so obvious to anyone who does it that its mysterious power is often mentioned in finance books that have no other spiritual or magical components at all. Larry Winget, in his book You're Broke Because You Want to Be, notes, "When you share what you have earned with others, then it magically comes back to you. I don't know why it works, but it works."

Time

Money is linked to time, and if you want to build wealth, you need to understand the relationship between the two. If you have ever worked at a company and were paid by the hour, chances are you worked for people who were paid a straight salary, and even though their paycheck was bigger than yours, they complained that when you really look at it, they make less. This is because in terms of relative income, they did make less. By working salary they probably put in a lot of overtime that they did not get paid extra for, and thus when you divide their salary by hours worked, they make less per hour.

This concept of time and money can be even more important when you own your own business. For many the entrepreneurial American dream turns out to be a trap that keeps them working almost nonstop. Even when you're not directly putting in hours, a business you own can occupy your thoughts in ways that truly make it a 24-hour job.

When planning a new career or business venture, you need to be careful and plot out time as well as money. Your career might very well give you a huge income, but if you spend 90 hours a week working, is that really what you want? Money and time need to be in balance.

People

The last quality that I want to share about the spirit of money is that money is linked to people. The people you know and surround yourself with can help open up opportunities for increasing your prosperity—or they can hold you back.

As you embark on the path of financial sorcery, you should take a second look at the people in your life and how they affect you. Make no mistake: Everyone in your life affects you both in terms of what happens around you and your own psychological makeup. You will find that some people in your life will be threatened by the idea of you making more money. Some will interpret any attempt to better yourself as a betrayal of working-class roots or a rejection of your heritage. You will find some friends accusing you of thinking that you are better than them or of acting "high and mighty."

When people know you as one thing, it is natural for them to act strangely when you become another. This goes not only for improving finances, but also for losing weight, as well as any other change in your life. People who are comforted by having a poor, fat friend (who makes them feel good by comparison) can easily be threatened by a rich, healthy friend.

On the other hand, having people in your life who know about money and investing and who have connections, can open up doorways to newer and greater experiences. About 70 percent of all jobs in America are filled through interpersonal connections, and most knowledge that people possess comes from other people. Investments, funds, jobs, negotiations—pretty much everything revolves around interpersonal relations. The ability to work with people, to influence, to befriend, and to help runs through everything that affects money.

x x x

These are the essential qualities of money as I see them. Are they the actual qualities of a living spirit, or is that just a fancy way of explaining the qualities of money? The truth is, I don't know, and it doesn't matter: Money behaves like a spirit that has these special qualities. That is all that matters. And knowing these qualities, we can now work on our skills.

Chapter 3

CORE SKILLS

D oing magic well is more than just speaking the right names, facing the right direction, and mixing the right herbs. Doing a spell here and there is easy enough, but implementing a full-scale magical strategy requires a certain level of skill. Most serious practitioners have a daily practice that keeps their skill set sharp. The more you work on it, the better you will get, just as with any other practice.

In my book The Sorcerer's Secrets, I presented a host of breath exercises, gazes, and regular practices for the general practitioner. In this chapter I will be focusing only on those exercises that I feel give the most bang for the buck in terms of results vs. time. For those involved in very traditional paths, it may seem strange to think about spiritual practices in terms of efficiency, but if we are to fully live in the world and have a meaningful magical practice, that is exactly what we need to do. Starting with meditation.

Meditation

Ralph Waldo Emerson once said, "The ancestor of every action is a thought." Everything you do in magic follows the mind. Mind drives the chariot of body and spirit, and meditation, a mental exercise, is the cornerstone of all the magic that I teach. If I had to give up all magical and spiritual disciplines except one, I would happily ditch everything else in favor of simple meditation.

Now, let me clarify what I mean by meditation, because it can mean a lot of things. It is defined simply as "to engage in mental exercise for spiritual purposes," which covers a lot of ground. Whereas, technically, kneeling in prayer, doing Tai Chi, or lying on the bed and listening to Enya could be considered meditation, they are not what I mean by meditation.

Meditation for me is a process for alleviating the grasping at thoughts and cutting through mental distractions to reveal a deeper and truer layer of awareness. There are many methods for this, but most of them boil down to focusing on a single thing and allowing all other thoughts to rise and set without engaging them. In short, it means sitting down and shutting up.

The problem is that sitting down and shutting up can be quite difficult. We are not wired for it. Magicians and witches in particular have a real problem with meditation. It goes against a lot of what we like about magic:

x Magicians like to do stuff. We like to chant, dance, make gestures, and so on. Meditation distinctly lacks the doing of stuff.

x Magicians like to see visions and be visited by spirits. Meditation instructs you to ignore those visions and politely tell the spirits and gods that show up to please leave you alone because you are meditating.

x Magicians like to experience and explore altered states of consciousness. Though meditation can cause these states, at its root it is actually all about your Normal State consciousness.

Note particularly that last point: Meditation has nothing to do with reaching altered states of consciousness. It only has to do with getting to know your own mind in its most normal and fundamental state. Getting to know your mind can help you reach altered states simply because you know your mind so well. It can also help you reach relaxed states, empathic states, or just about any other state of mind that you choose because it is not a type of trance or altered state in and of itself.

In the beginning stages of meditation, you are focusing on one thing. This lasts for seconds before you get distracted. You then gently return to the meditation. That's it, at first. If you are doing anything else, then you are distracted. If you are having visions of Gabriel or the Goddess or anything else, you are distracted. Meditation is the practice of cutting through distraction.

Some people who try to meditate decide they are bad at it and give up. Some claim outright that they cannot do it; they tell me that they tried in the past and couldn't "get there" or "clear their minds." They would like to meditate, but they stink at it. Perhaps you are one of these people. If so, I have some good news for you.

You cannot be bad at meditation.

Barring serious mental illness,[1] everyone can meditate. The problem many people have can be summed up as one of expectation and tenacity: The expectation of what is "supposed to" occur in meditation is often a lot grander than what actually happens. People expect that they will sit down and the mind will quickly quiet and stay perfectly still for the length of the session. They expect to feel a calming peace that they have never felt before and will be one with everything. These expectations are unrealistic, especially when the subject is willing to give all of three sessions of effort toward the goal before declaring that they cannot meditate. This lack of tenacity is even worse than the unrealistic expectation.

Part of the reason people throw in the towel so quickly is that during their first few sessions, they are surprised at how little control they have over their mind. Most people feel as though they have a good handle on themselves; they are successful, smart, and healthy, and generally feel in control of their lives. It can be a pretty big shock to find out that they cannot focus on one thing exclusively even for one minute. Something seemingly so easy and so basic as directing your own thoughts should not be this hard, they think. They judge themselves and feel embarrassed at their lack of control and quickly abandon the practice.

The first thing to do when undertaking meditation is to abandon any desire for results. You should expect to be distracted almost constantly. In fact, if you are keeping a regular practice of meditating every day, you should expect nothing but distraction for at least six months! You sit and focus on breath, or on mantra or yantra, and a thought of food arises in the mind stream. You start thinking about dinner. This gets you thinking about the time, and wondering how much time has passed so far. You realize that you have lost focus.

This is the crucial moment. When you recognize that you are distracted, the natural reaction is to berate yourself because you stopped meditating. The secret is this: You didn't stop meditating. You recognized your distraction: That is meditation. If you can then return to focusing without judgment, you will continue to meditate properly. If you willingly continue to be distracted, knowing that you are distracted, now you have stopped meditating.

If you spend your whole life experiencing nothing in your meditation sessions other than being distracted and returning to the focus of the meditation, you will have accomplished quite a lot. You will have mastered your own thought process. I cannot stress enough what a wonderful feat this is. Almost everything that people do, say, and think is just a mechanical reaction. How you were raised, what you ate for breakfast, what traffic was like, what genes you inherited, how you are dressed—all these things impact every moment of our lives and push us one way or another. If you can recognize the mind being distracted by a habitual pattern in meditation, you will learn to recognize these patterns in everyday life. The next time someone pushes your buttons and you start to react, you will probably catch yourself and react from a place of real thought rather than of habit. Good job!

So what does this have to do with financial sorcery specifically? Why is this the most important skill to master? Because everything that is really important in transforming yourself financially boils down to being able to do things that go against your immediate desires and instincts. Examples:

x Debt happens because people want the immediate reward that a purchase gives and are willing to pay the price later. People kill their debt by forcing themselves to do what they know to be right in the face of those immediate desires.

x People reach retirement age without any savings because they prefer to have as much money as possible from their current paycheck available now. People save for retirement by overcoming that instinct and saving and investing that money, doing without the immediate rewards.

x Warren Buffett has noted that people who win in the stock market are those who can buy when everyone is selling. Those who lose are those who bought what everyone thinks is a great deal (and is therefore high-priced), and sell when recessions hit, rather than sticking it out or taking advantage of low prices and investing more.

In all three cases, it is control of your mind that is key. Recognize distraction, release yourself from it, and return to what it is that you will yourself to accomplish. This is the first gift of meditation. Eventually, with practice, you will probably experience some genuine subtle states such as Rigpa or Samadhi, as described in classical texts, but these come with time and must not be sought after directly. Even if you do not experience these states, you will have accomplished much just by taking a little bit of control over your own mind.

Just remember that you cannot be bad at it. If the point is to recognize distraction, what is there to be bad at? Eventually you stop being distracted as easily. You win the battle against wandering trains of thought, you win the battle against agitation, and you win the battle against dullness. Now you drop even the focus of the meditation and are able to just be clear, naturally and effortlessly.

Breath

There is a reason that in many cultures, the word for spirit or energy is also the word for breath. In Hebrew the word is ruach, in Tibetan it's lung, in Sanskrit it's prana, in Greek it's pneuma, and in Arabic it's ruh. Even the word spirit or spiritus itself means "breath" in Latin. The breath is life and is so important that it is treated in some Eastern traditions as a mantra in and of itself. Yet we pay surprisingly little attention to it.

From the beginning, breath is neglected. Right at the moment of birth the doctor usually cuts the umbilical cord before the lungs have had a chance to clear the fluid that has built up in the lungs in utero. Our first breaths in this life are breaths of panic and fear, a trauma that some say we never quite recover from, and thus remain afraid of taking a full and complete breath.

Under normal circumstances people only use about one-seventh of their lung capacity, taking in only one pint of air approximately 15 times per minute. When we are excited or frightened we breathe even faster and shorter, which heightens our state of fear. This response does have an evolutionary role in keeping us safe from danger, but in our modern world this reflex kicks in under all kinds of stress that does not involve actual danger, and in which a cooler head would be of more benefit.

The breath is an autonomic function; it happens automatically, similar to your heartbeat and digestive function. Of all the autonomic systems, the breath is the easiest to take voluntary control of and is thus an excellent vehicle to bridge the gap between the conscious and subconscious mind. The breath usually follows whatever state your mind happens to be in, but it's easy to reverse the process and make the mind follow the breath instead.

A number of different breath techniques can be employed in magic. I wrote at great length about some of them in The Sorcerer's Secrets, but there is one basic technique that is important to master for the work at hand: the vase breath.

The Vase Breath

The vase breath is so named because with this method you are filling your lungs the way you would fill a vase with water: from the bottom up. As I mentioned, the lungs will hold about seven pints of air, yet we generally only draw in one pint at a time. We also tend to favor the upper chambers of the lungs, puffing out our chests and holding in our stomachs. Although this may be a more physically attractive way of breathing, it's not very efficient.

To perform the vase breath, you must make sure that your back is reasonably straight and vertical. Sitting or standing are both fine, but do not do it lying down. Then simply breathe in through the nostrils, keeping the mouth closed and filling the lower chambers of the lungs first. Allow the belly to distend as you do this. Then allow the upper chambers of the lungs to fill almost all the way. You should aim to take in about six pints of air. If you do this correctly your breath rate should slow from about 15 times per minute to about 8 times per minute.

When the vase breath is used, the flow of oxygen to the blood and brain is improved, which has many benefits. One of the primary benefits is that the pituitary gland begins to function optimally. This gland controls all the other glands in the body, and is also the physical manifestation of the third eye and the seat of mystical vision. If you are sensitive to the energies of the body, you will also note an increased flow of vital force in the body as well as an improved ability to direct these energies using only the breath and the will.

Even more important, just as meditation trains the mind to release distraction and recall your true will, the vase breath can act as the key to actually doing this in the moment: By forcing the breath into a slow and full inhalation, we are signaling the mind to calm down and return to the state that it is usually in when we are breathing that way—calm and clear.

The Pillar

This exercise can be done sitting or standing, but both positions should be mastered. In both cases the back should be held as straight as possible. Begin to perform the vase breath. Then pull in a deep inhalation and imagine that above you, emanating from the highest heavens, descends a column of pure white light. This light enters the crown of your head and passes through you, down into the ground. This white light is ennobling and purifying.

Pull in another deep inhalation and imagine that a reddish-colored light rises from beneath you, continues up through the column, and passes through you out of the crown of your head. Whereas the white light was purifying, this light is vivifying. As the descending light was ennobling, this energy is atavistic. Inhale and feel the two energies entering into you from above and below. Exhale and feel the two energies flow throughout your body, impregnating every fiber of your being with their power. Feel your connection between earth and sky, underworld and heavens.

One sign that you have mastered this practice is that when you are walking and performing the pillar exercise you will feel as though you are staying in one spot and the world is moving around you, like a figure in a video game.

The Spheres

Do the pillar exercise just described, and then turn your attention to the crown of your head. Imagine an empty sphere that extends inside and above your skull. Breathe in and see a clear energy fill this sphere. It corresponds to the element Azoth, which is spirit and space and brings increased clarity and spacious awareness. Move the mind downward and see a sphere at the throat. Breathe in an airy, bright yellow energy that feels warm and wet like humid air and moves about rapidly within the sphere. Move the mind downward again to a sphere at the heart. Breathe in a deep blue energy that feels cool and fluid. Move the mind downward to a sphere just below and behind the navel near the base of the spine. Breathe a red, hot, dry, and expansive energy into this sphere. Move the mind downward again to the perineum between the legs, behind the genitals. See a dark, earth-tone energy that is dense, cool, and dry fill this sphere. Rest the mind a few minutes and contemplate the elements within the body.

The purpose of this exercise is to balance the five elements along the central channel, which is the most important psychic structure in the subtle body. This not only mends energetic imbalances that can cause various physical and emotional ills, but also sets them up in a specific alchemical order. You could imagine the classical view of a witch's cauldron or an alchemical vial within the body. The earth is the ground that the fire is built upon. The fire boils the water in the cauldron or vial above it; the boiled water releases steam into the air; the steam ascends to the heavens and dissipates into space.

Many internal energy exercises are built upon this pattern, but for our purposes here, you simply need to be able to balance the energies of the body, which are also connected intimately to the mind and the emotions.

Intelligence Gathering

Divination is the most commonly performed type of magic on the planet, and any of us who have ever read our horoscope in the newspaper, shaken a Magic 8-Ball, or predicted bad luck when a black cat crossed our path has engaged in it on one level or another. Thousands of psychics and readers are consulted every day, all over the world, by people from all walks of life, on topics ranging from lost loves to matters of state. It has been so since the beginning of human history. The Chinese have been using the I-Ching since 1000 BC, making it one of the oldest types of divination on the planet. Babylonian kings, Roman generals, and even one pope have relied upon haruspices, or diviners, to read the entrails and livers of sacrificed animals before battle. Divination is widely practiced for sure...but there is a problem.

When I give classes on divination I start out by asking whether people have ever had a reading before, and almost everyone has. I then ask how many times they have actually made a life-altering decision based on such a reading. Very few hands have ever been raised. The problem is that one reading, no matter how good, is rarely considered to be actionable information. In intelligence communities this is the combination of intel and data. Intel is information that has been evaluated more for its relevancy to active situations than for its accuracy. Data, on the other hand, are seen as particular units of verifiable information, regardless of their current application. Whenever we receive information from any source, be it rumors at work or a tarot reading, it is vital to evaluate it for both its relevancy and its accuracy. In serious situations, several types of divination from different sources should be consulted in order to get a full picture. If an effort can be made to verify the information by non-magical methods, all the better.

For instance, a tarot reading that you perform about the possibility of your being laid off is relevant, but may not be very accurate. If you get your results confirmed by several other readers, the probability of accuracy goes up. If you get those further backed up by some office rumors, you now have some actionable intelligence on which to base a decision.

I am not going to tell you how to perform readings; chances are you already know how to do that. What I do want to warn about is trusting just one reading when making decisions. The fact is that no matter how good a reader is, he or she can be wrong. And when you are reading for yourself, your own desires can influence your interpretation.

In order to help create intelligence in which you can be confident enough to act upon, I recommend mastering three different modes of divination, such as sortilege with tarot cards or runes, augury in something like candle wax or bones, and the interpretation of omens and dreams. When you couple these skills with keen observation (and also the ability to get people to share inside information with you), you can be much more confident in your intelligence.

Keeping an Altar

The last skill that I want to discuss here is that of creating and keeping an altar. Unlike some other issues that you may tackle occasionally with sorcery, such as finding a lover or dealing with a court case, you will be dealing with financial issues until the day you die. Even if you manage to strike it filthy rich, you will need to manage your money wisely. Because of this, many sorcerers find it useful to erect permanent wealth altars.

It might seem odd to think of tending an altar as a skill, but it is. Whether it's a large and ornate altar worthy of a temple, or a discreet corner of a bookshelf, a permanent altar acts as a psychic control panel for your life. Symbolic items placed upon the altar will manifest— even those placed there accidentally, which means that dust on the altar will create dust in your life. Using an altar is a great way to keep long-term spells going and coordinate strategies, but if you don't keep it up, it is best not to do it at all.

To make your own altar, simply decide how much space you can afford to devote to it, and then clean off this area. Place a green, blue, or gold altar cloth on it to demarcate the space as sacred. Place any wealth-related effigies, amulets, talismans, or sorcerous paraphernalia on the altar and arrange them according to your inner guidance. Perform a brief consecration of your own devising.

Among the items on my financial altar are:

x A large print of Dzambhala, the Buddhist deity of wealth

x A print of White Mahakala, a Tibetan wish-granting deity that overcomes obstacles

x A statue of Mary with a Miraculous Medal I was given by my grandmother

x A picture of my grandfather, who was a successful businessman

x Several green and gold candles burning for various clients

x A Jupiterian cashbox (which I will describe in a later chapter)

x A box with a string of sigils[2] etched into it containing banking information on various investments x Spirit bottles for Marie Laveau and Dr. John, the most famous and prosperous Voodoo practitioners in New Orleans, for influencing money I receive from doing magical work

x My year-long petition (for whatever I hope to gain in the new year) and lodestone

x A Rose of Jericho (a dry, desert plant that turns green and unfolds in water), used to absorb negativity, in a bowl of water that gets changed every Friday

No matter how elaborate your altar, everything on it should be clean and meaningful. Nothing can be placed there that doesn't have a purpose. I don't care if the rest of your home is a filthy hoarder disaster waiting for an HGTV crew to clean it up—your altar must be clean and nothing on it should be left to rot. If there is liquid in anything (oil lamps, water bowls, and so on) they must be changed regularly. If there is incense, the ash must be taken care of regularly. Treat it like a living thing, because on an esoteric level, that is exactly what it is.

x x x

Now that we have talked about the basic skills you will need going forward, it is time to meet and greet the powers that be!

References and Resources

The Sorcerer's Secrets: Strategies in Practical Magick, by Jason Miller (New Page Books, August 2009): My previous book, which goes into more detail about the skills mentioned in this chapter, as well as other subtle keys to magic that you may find useful.

The Strategic Sorcery Course, taught by Jason Miller. This is a 52-lesson course in practical magic. If you like The Sorcerer's Secrets, this is the next step.

Meditation in a New York Minute: Super Calm for the Super Busy, an audiobook by Mark Thornton (Sounds

True, Inc., February 1, 2006). This is probably the best book on meditation for those who are not involved in a particular meditative tradition such as Buddhism. It is straight, to the point, easily adapted to modern life, and focuses on the most important practices.

Mystical Origins of the Tarot: From Ancient Roots to Modern Usage, by Paul Huson (Destiny Books, May 26, 2004). The best book on tarot, period.

Chapter 4

THE POWERS THAT BE

The sorcerer does not work in a vacuum. Spirits, angels, demons, gods, and all manner of beings will be called upon during the course of your career. Some you will pray to fervently for help, others you will merely name in spells, and some you will attempt to communicate with directly. This chapter is a quick overview of some types of beings you may interact with during the course of a financial sorcery strategy. It is by no means complete, or in any way comprehensive, as doing so would fill several books.

Local Beings and Regular Offerings

I believe that the best place for the sorcerer to start building relationships with spirits is not with the angels and demons of famous grimoires or the gods of various religions, but with the local beings in the places where one lives, works, and plays. You probably don't know the names of these beings; most of them do not even have names. In some cases we are talking about powers that blend with one another in ways that can be perplexing.

There are beings of the sky, of the land, of the rivers, of the underworld, and even of electricity and cities. There are great angelic powers, spirit guardians, shades of the dead, dryadic spirits, and all manner of beings with which you share space and generally do not interact with in conscious ways. In many cases such beings are thought to have influence on wealth and prosperity in your life. In Tibet many people offer Sang (smoke offerings, usually of juniper and pine) to the Nagas and the Shidak to help increase their flow of prosperity. In India similar rites are done to appease the Yakshas and Yashninis, for similar reasons. In Iceland there are areas where the government demands that a shaman come and tell whether the Huldufolk (elves) would be upset by your actions and thus negatively impact business all around.

You do not need to get excessively particular about names and classes in order to make things run smoothly for you with the local spirits. I certainly do encourage you to research your area both psychic-ally and historically, but to get started it is enough to make a general offering on a regular basis to the powers that be.

The type of offering I am talking about here is not one in which you ask for anything in exchange. What I am talking about is an act of spiritual kindness. If you make these offerings a part of your regular practice, then you will develop more powerful and longer-term relationships with the spirits than you do with simple tit-for-tat contracts.

Think of it this way: If you needed $50 and you asked a complete stranger to loan it to you they would probably say no. If you asked people with whom you work for $50, they may lend it or they may not. If you asked your best friend for $50, it's almost certain that he or she would lend it and then ask if you needed anything else. Your friend would also probably not be as concerned about the date of payback because you have a long history with this person, likely making gestures of goodwill to one another for years.

In my Strategic Sorcery Course I place a great deal of emphasis on offerings, and I have an elaborate classification system for different guests and levels of offerings that can be made for different reasons. For our purposes here it is enough to know that you are making an offering to just about every spirit that would like to show up and partake, from the meekest spirit of nature to the greatest godly power; from beings that are your spirit allies and patrons to those that might be angry with you.

Some people might feel uncomfortable with the idea of making offerings to spirits that are angry with them and might be considered enemies, but in fact nothing is more traditional—or important to do! One of the oldest manifestations of the healing arts on this planet is the art of healing the differences between people and spirits. The most common example is a spirit of nature that you've angered through your ordinary human actions, such as driving or getting rid of trash. Being a magician, you are even more apt to trample upon the turf of spirits or powers of which you may not even be aware. This is one of the dangers of the endless banishing rituals sometimes recommended in books on ceremonial magic. In the process of financial sorcery it is just as important to pacify angry spirits as it is to make friends with new ones.

In order to get this practice working in your life you should first decide upon a time of day and a frequency of offering. People usually perform offerings early in the morning, if not very first thing. I make them daily, but some people will only be comfortable making offerings weekly. Others I know make offerings three times a day to attract different spirits focused on the morning, midday, and night. You should plan on doing as much as you can, but no more than that. Be realistic. It is better to make a regular weekly offering on Thursday mornings than it is to be gung-ho about elaborate daily offerings three times a day for a few days, then fall off the wagon completely because you have chosen a plan that does not fit your lifestyle.

After the frequency is decided, you should plan what kind of physical support you will use. You can make offerings of energy with no physical support, but I reserve these for moments when I am inspired to make an offering on the fly, such as before I sit and meditate at a city park, or when I am traveling and do not have access to gear. For your regular offerings I recommend having a physical support that will ground your work in our physical reality and open up the lines of communication between you and the spirits.

I recommend the following types of support:

1. **Incense:** Incense is a great support for physical offerings. The ascending smoke is not only said to carry one's prayers to the higher realms, but to also actually be consumed by classes of beings called "scent eaters."

2. **Light:** Light is a nearly universal symbol for wisdom. It is appreciated by most spiritual beings and is thought to actually be consumed by certain beings. I prefer candles and actual fire to electric light, but some beings have come to appreciate that as well. (I never leave candles burning unattended in my home, so sometimes electricity is what I need, like it or not.) Whatever you use as an offering should be separate from your work lights—the lights you use to illuminate your temple. Offering lights are dedicated as offerings only.

3. **Water:** Water symbolizes purity and washing clean. It is an extremely attractive and calming substance for many spirits to linger near, especially spirits of the dead. Setting out one, three, seven, or more bowls of clean water in the morning and emptying them at night is a wonderful offering.

4. **Libation:** In addition to water in a bowl you can offer water, tea, coffee, or another liquid to the ground.

I try, whenever possible, to offer all four on a regular basis. The upward rising of the incense, the outward rays of the light, the stationary bowl of water, and the downward flow of the libation are nice symbols for extending your offering. Whatever the physical base used, you should also multiply it by visualization and energy. In this manner, no matter what the physical basis, it can be patterned to fit the needs of any and all beings.

If you get really into the practice of offering and have the space, you can get more elaborate by putting out fruit, flowers, meat, money, objects, and more. Skilled people can also use sacred acts such as sex as an offering, but in most cases these would not be for a regular and general offering like what I am describing here.

You must be careful when offering to specific classes of spirits or individual spirits. Research the traditions carefully and then use that knowledge to make an appropriate offering. Then listen to the spirits and see if they ask for something specific. Some offerings, such as meat or musk to Nagas and salt to spirits of the dead, can actually offend a guest and make the ritual counterproductive. If you aren't sure of what you are doing, stick to the basic gesture of offering, with simple substances such as incense and liquor.

A Daily Offering to the Spirits for Financial Wellness

In my last book, The Sorcerer's Secrets, I included a good general offering, and in my Strategic Sorcery Course I give another, more elaborate example as well as different variations that can be made. In this book I wanted to include something that was even shorter than what I put into The Sorcerer's Secrets but which also has an eye toward the financial dimension.

There are three segments to a proper offering: the invitation, the offering itself, and the dismissal. When using physical supports, these three should be preceded by a cleansing or blessing of the material to be offered, making it a four-stage ritual.

The following simple ritual follows these four stages:

Cleansing

By Earth, the body of the Gods

By Water, their flowing blood

By Air, the breath of the Gods

By Fire, their burning soul

May these offerings be made blessed and made pure.

Invitation

Aeon of Aeons, Bornless and Perfected Ones;

Angels and Archons and Guardians of the Work;

Every God of Celestial Spheres;

Phantoms of the Dead, the Quick, and in between;

Every spirit of the Earth, the Air, and the Underworld;

Every spirit who causes harm in response to human action,

In particular you Gods and Spirits who oversee the flow and gathering of wealth;

Spirits of luck and opportunity;

Spirits of accretion and affluence:

Come here according to your desires. And be seated upon the thrones.

Offering

During this portion of the rite you make your actual offering. Light your incense and wave it about in the air; hold your candles out to symbolically offer their illumination; pour your libations on the ground; place your items at the altar, or, in the case of making offerings to beings to which you owe debt, move the offerings outside the temple.

Clouds of offerings, I give to you

Food and drink and fumigation.

Let the offerings arise and pervade all space.

Let it take the form that is most desired.

Know that I am thankful for your past kindnesses.

Know that I am regretful for any offenses.

Please accept these offerings and be fulfilled.

Please open the paths of prosperity

And meet kindness with kindness.

Dismissal

Please take your fill of these offerings and go in peace.

Go unto your abodes as you desire.

Forever act as friends and helpers.

So Mote It Be.

Amen.

Spirits of the Financially Savvy Dead

Your ancestors may have passed on, but they may still prove to be some of your most powerful allies. They live on in us, in our very blood. Acknowledgment of your ancestors with an occasional offering is a great way to contact beings to whom you already have a psychic connection, and who will almost always be inclined to help you. There is a reason that in many African traditional religions, getting in touch with one's ancestors is the first step on the path. If someone in your family was known as a magician or psychic, that would be a good person to start with.

Contacting your ancestors can be simple and rewarding. You can lay out a simple bowl of water and a white candle, or go further and set up a proper Boveda. This is a table with a white cloth upon which is set a cross or other symbol of divinity, a white candle, and a center bowl or glass of water surrounded by seven other smaller cups of water. Once a week you set aside an hour or so to set out gifts such as coffee or food that your ancestors enjoyed in life, raise the bowls, and sing praises to them. Even if you are not of their religion, saying prayers that would be meaningful to them is more important than acknowledging your own beliefs. If you want to do a weeklong offering you can raise one of the glasses in their honor each day, telling them that as you do so you are lifting your spirit to them. On the last day, when you are doing the last bowl or cup, you should open yourself up and look for any feelings or messages that come through. This process opens a portal to the convocation of spirits in your bloodline. You may discover ancestors and spirit guides presenting themselves that you never even knew you had. I discovered a twin that died as an infant on my father's side this way, which I later confirmed with my grandmother.

If you get a particularly strong connection, you can create an ancestor altar where you house pictures and belongings. You can also gather graveyard dirt from their resting place, and use it in spells for your financial strategies. Both of my own grandfathers were shrewd businessmen whom I am honored to have as allies in my work.

Apart from your ancestors it can sometimes be helpful to call upon the spirits of deceased community members or coworkers in the course of your rituals. The founder of the company where you work, for instance, can be a very potent ally for gaining promotion, and a recently deceased council member can help grease the wheels of local government for that new business you want to open.

Working with the dead is not for everyone. Some people consider it best to leave those who have passed alone, so that they can continue their journey without undue attachment to a former life. Others would never think of abandoning their ancestors and believe it would be an offense to the dead to leave them be. I am not interested in arguing one point over the other here. If you decide to work with the dead, it can be rewarding. If you decide not to, there are plenty of other options.

Planetary Powers

In *The Sorcerer's Secrets* I point out that although many people think of Jupiter as the only planet/god to invoke in money matters, if you are doing real financial sorcery you should be a little more nuanced in your thinking. In that book I suggest working with a Jupiter/Mercury combo—Jupiter handing the collection of money and Mercury handling its movement, sort of the way your savings and checking accounts complement each other. If you are really intending to become a financial sorcerer, though, you should consider the role of all the planets in your work.

A few years ago on the Strategic Sorcery Blog, I issued "Inominandum's Two-Week Planetary Challenge," in which you would consider a goal you are working toward and factor each planet's influence into your strategy by invoking the power of each planet on its proper day and hour. If you start on a Monday and perform an invocation every other day, you will move through all the planets in their ascending Chaldean order (Monday: moon; Wednesday: Mercury; Friday: Venus; Sunday: sun; Tuesday: Mars; Thursday: Jupiter; Saturday: Saturn) in two weeks.

Of course there are a lot of ways to approach planetary work. You can invoke the Roman gods they are named after; you can call them by the names of the Archangels, or the intelligences and spirits from Agrippa, or the Olympic spirits from the Arbatel, or even the Babylonian/Sumerian gods associated with them. The following is a quick reference chart for some of the more common planetary correspondences.[1]

ROMAN GOD/ PLANET	DAY OF THE WEEK	ARCHANGEL	INTELLIGENCE OF THE PLANET	SPIRIT OF THE PLANET	OLYMPIC SPIRIT	SUMERIAN/ BABYLONIAN
Saturn	Saturday	Tzaphkiel	Agiel	Zazel	Aratron	Ninib
Jupiter	Thursday	Tzadkiel	Iophiel	Hismael	Bethor	Marduk
Mars	Tuesday	Khammael	Nakhiel	Bartzabel	Phaleg	Nergal
Sol	Sunday	Michael	Graphiel	Sorath	Och	Shammash
Venus	Friday	Haniel	Hagiel	Kedemel	Hagith	Inanna
Mercury	Wednesday	Raphael	Tiriel	Taphtharthath	Ophiel	Nebo
Luna	Monday	Gabriel		Chashmodai	Phul	Nanna

Sample of Planetary Correspondences

I actually hate charts like this one. All too often people feel the need to use all the names for a particular planet in a single invocation, as if the sheer amount of different sources and cultures somehow lent it power. I provide this list only as a place to start looking for more pertinent information. In each column there are different names you should be researching to either follow a traditional rite or construct your own based on those names. It is far better to wax poetic about how Tzadkiel charges into battle right behind Michael, leads the Choir of Dominions, and prevents Abraham from sacrificing Isaac, than it is to yell out, "Iovis, Mustari, Tzadkiel, Iophiel, Hismael, Bethor, Marduk, be here now!" The former method attracts and deepens the connection with a particular power; the latter creates a crowded mess, if it does anything at all.

So how do all the planets impact your work? Let's give an example—say you want to land a job:

Luna: The moon is often misunderstood as a planet that is only about deep instinct, women's mysteries, dreams, and such. But it is also about time and rhythm. For ancient peoples the most obvious and easiest way to track days was by the phases of the moon. The tides and some bodily functions also flow with the moon. Tibetans believe that there are certain key Bindus, or drops, that flow through different parts of the body based on a lunar schedule, and to work yoga correctly you need to know where those are. So, if you want your strategy to put you in the right place at the right time, this is an ideal place to start. In our case we might call upon Luna to help us make sure that we are looking at the right time to see the ideal job offerings, and to make sure that our applications also hit at the appropriate time.

Mercury: As I have already mentioned, Mercury is about movement and information. Because you will be applying for a lot of jobs online, you had better have the powers of information in your corner!

Venus: Venus is all about interpersonal communications and bringing people together. Invoke the powers of Venus before you network with friends, former coworkers, and networking groups. Invoke them again before the job interview to sweeten relations.

Sol: The sun calls to mind harmony, divine guidance, health, and sudden bursts of energy and inspiration. If you are stuck in a rut and need to see a different approach to your job search, the sun can help shed light on paths you had not considered. It is also invoked by people looking for patrons and helpers.

Mars: Let's face it: there is steep competition out there for just about everything. Mars helps you cut through this and arise victorious. You may invoke Mars to banish your bad luck or crossed conditions. You may invoke him to give you an air of command before an interview. If things get dire, Mars can be invoked in more wrathful ways as well. I personally think that problems are best handled as peacefully as possible, but business is business, and not all business is nice. Certainly, given the history of magic and witchcraft, nothing could be more traditional.

Jupiter: Jupiter is associated with increase, riches, and wealth, and also has roles that can sometimes overlap with other powers, such as making war, and lust. Use Jupiter to make sure that your upcoming job pays the salary and has the benefits that you need. I'll talk more about Jupiter in the next chapter.

Saturn: Saturn is your end game. Invoke him to end projects the way you want them to. Just as you banished your bad luck with Mars, you can kill your poverty with Saturn. Saturn is also for binding, so if you find yourself distracted or not making the most of your time, Saturn might be the power to turn to. You can also banish Saturn if you feel its influence weighing you down. Very skilled sorcerers who are used to mediating these influences can both invoke and banish Saturnian influences at the same time, keeping the parts they want and banishing those they do not—but such talents are only conferred by experience and cannot be properly explained in a book.

Those who are deep into astrology will want to not only choose the right day and hour, but also abide by a host of other electional conditions. If you want to go further, I strongly recommend the classes and books of Christopher Warnock at Renaissance Astrology.

A Miscellany of Spirits and Dieties: Furthering Your Financial Network

It is truly dizzying how many different spirits get invoked in financial magic the world over. Some are general and some are laser-focused. Following is just a quick miscellany of beings I have worked with successfully. Do some research before working with any of them. The blurbs I've provided are just meant to whet your appetite. Let's kick things off with some saints:

Saint Expedite: St. Expedite was a Roman soldier and is the patron saint of getting things done quickly. If you have any interest in folk magic at all, chances are you already know all about him. If you belong to a hoodoo or folk magic mailing list, you will see posts thanking him for all kinds of last-minute saves. Those public statements of gratitude, along with a slice of poundcake, are all the offerings St. Expedite needs to help you out with your last-minute needs. He is so popular that there are articles about him in Wired and other mainstream magazines. A word of warning: Do not ask him to do what is simply impossible in a short amount of time, and do not demand his swift action on things that do not need it—his energy will spill all over your life in unpleasant ways.

Saint Homobonus: A merchant from Cremona in Italy, he believed that God allowed his success in order for him to support the poor. He is very responsive when approached with business deals in which you promise to dedicate a small percentage of profits to the poor. Although he is not a popular saint, even among Catholics, I have actually seen cheap plastic statues of him made by a toy company, and there is also a marketing agency in Cambridge, England, named after him.

Saint Jude: This is the very well known saint of impossible causes and last-ditch efforts. If you are nearing the end of your unemployment insurance, if your business is on the verge of bankruptcy, or if your portfolio has lost 50 percent of its worth and you are 60 years old, St. Jude might be your guy.

Our Lady of the Miraculous Medal: My grandmother introduced me to this form of Mary, and she has proven exceptionally reliable. In 1830 the Virgin appeared to St. Catherine Laboure and instructed her on the construction of a very specific medal that would benefit humanity. I had mine blessed at the Miraculous Medal Shrine in Philadelphia, and she has acted in good faith whenever I have called on her. There are Novenas for all sorts of intercessions connected with her, but many people are currently looking to her for help with employment.

Our Lady of Prompt Succor: This is a form of Mary that is especially connected with New Orleans, a city I dearly love. She helped turn the tide of battle when she appeared in the sky above the Battle of New Orleans, and has been called upon to save the city from hurricanes and other disasters many times over throughout the last few hundred years. Similar to St. Expedite, she is known to work quickly. I myself have had small requests granted the very hour that the request was made.

Dzambhala: Moving east, we have one of my favorite wealth-building figures. Dzambhala, also spelled Jambhala, is a Tibetan/Indian deity of increase and prosperity. There are actually five different-colored Dzambhalas associated with the five Buddha families and different types of magical action. In all forms he possesses a large, rotund body and, like almost all Tibetan wealth deities, carries a mongoose that vomits gems. Yellow Dzambhala is the most prevalent form and is more or less a straightforward wealth deity. Black Dzambhala is wrathful and overcomes obstacles. White Dzambhala is very peaceful and compassionate. Blue Dzambhala operates primarily through spiritual means. Red Dzambhala increases wealth through influence and charm; he is sometimes shown as being in sexual union with Kurukulla, the goddess of influence and witchcraft.

White Mahakala: White Mahakala is a wrathful form of Avalokiteshvara, the Bodhisattva of Compassion. He is actually standing on two Ganeshas who hold the ubiquitous mongoose vomiting gems. He himself carries blades, wish-granting gems, a skull cup filled with jewels, and a hook of attraction. White Mahakala is specifically for overcoming obstacles, and I can testify that he does it with speed and style. As with most Tibetan beings, it is best if you get the mantra and empowerment from a Lama, but even if you do not have such an initiation, you can still pray and make a request to the being.

Ganesha: Everybody loves Ganesha, and there is more than enough information about him out there. He is not only connected with overcoming obstacles, but with gambling as well. Om Gam Ganapati Ye Namah is just one mantra that will connect you with this powerful god.

Mahalakshmi: Mahalakshmi, or just Lakshmi, is probably the preeminent Hindu goddess of wealth. She is the consort of Vishnu and is married to Rama in her incarnation as Sita. All of Krishna's wives were said to be manifestations of Lakshmi.

The 36 Yakshinis: Yakshas, which I've already mentioned briefly, are similar to gnomes: They are spirits widely acknowledged throughout Asia as guardians of national treasures. The Yakshas are portrayed mostly as warriors, and the females, or Yakshinis, are seen as sensual and beautiful full-figured women. The Yakshinis are a bit easier to work with than the Yakshas, and there are numerous pujas (rituals) for asking for their help. Specifically, there are 36 Yakshinis listed as a group in the Uddamershvara Tantra that can be called upon with specific mantras and pujas.

Maximon: Returning west, let's also head south to Guatemala, where we have a complex god with a quickly spreading cult: Maximon. He is a Mayan god of the underworld once known as Mam, whom locals have synchretized with St. Simon, thus the contraction Maximon. Local priests trying to dissuade locals from worshiping him have tried to identify him with Judas, but this has only lent him popularity.

He is often invoked for financial gain, and offered expensive ciga-
rettes, cigars, and whiskey. Many statues have holes for the god to
drink and smoke through. There are many complex rites and beliefs
about Maximon, but he is also open to approach from people who are
not from an area where he is widely worshiped and thus may not know
his traditional prayers. One interesting charm associated with him involves jars of the waste water collected from washing his clothes during the pre-Easter festival. The liquid is then blessed and sprinkled in
shop doorways to attract customers.

High John the Conqueror: Most people are familiar with the
root named after him, but not as many know that he can be invoked as
a powerful spirit in his own right. He is something of a trickster figure;
having been sold as a slave, all the stories revolve around him getting
the better of his masters. Some claim that Brer Rabbit of the Uncle
Remus stories is modeled after John the Conqueror. Considering that
Bugs Bunny was modeled after Brer Rabbit, this shape-shifting spirit
has done an amazing job of staying within the popular consciousness.
Call on him when holding a whole High John Root and ask him for his
clever help.

Green Devil: The devil is of course no stranger to magic. From
Satanic rites to sunrise meetings at the crossroads, he plays a huge
role in the history of magic and witchcraft. Those who refuse to see
this aspect of the Horned God are cutting themselves off from a major
mystery. He finds his way into this book as a spirit to invoke to get
people who owe you money to pay their debts. His candles are not
easy to find, but they can be dressed with compelling oil and a prayer
made to the Green Devil to plague your debtor until he pays his debt.
I used it on a company once and it worked just as surely as it does on
an individual.

Hertha: This is a German earth goddess that has been worshiped
by witches for centuries. All goddesses of the earth are fantastic
financial powers, representing the bounty of the earth and its treasures: literal gold.

Habondia: Daughter of Hertha, sometimes seen as the same being. Habondia is specifically connected with abundance and wealth. Bonus: There is a lending society that assists in financially empowering and educating women called The Circle of Habondia.

x x x

These are just a small sample of the deities and spirits I have worked with throughout the years. You should do additional research on them if you hope to work with them. You may also find many more deities and spirits to add to this list. Just remember the following rules.

Inominandum's Rules for Working With Spirits

Whatever beings you decide to call upon in your work, there are a few things to keep in mind.

1. **Depth is better than quantity.** It is better to extol the virtues and actions of one being in an invocation than to invoke many different gods and names. Just because they are prosperity or Jupiterian beings does not mean that they are the same. Even deities that are traditionally synchretized, such as Thoth-Hermes or Jupiter-Zeus, are not the same. Those synchretizations are pulling together two mythologies in a very particular way—something not to be undertaken lightly. I have been to too many open circles where the goal seems to be to call as many deities into each quarter as possible with absolutely no attempt made to learn much about any of them, other than their names. This is the kind of thing that gives eclecticism a bad name. Do some research to learn about the being. Follow this with experimentation and communication. Use what comes through for more research and experimentation.

2. **Personal relationship trumps association.** If you have a long and ongoing relationship with a spirit, saint, or deity, but it is

not necessarily a "wealth" being, you may be better off asking it for help than starting a new relationship with a wealth being. Many entities have more facets than we know, and can turn their special talents toward your goal. One student of mine has worked almost exclusively with Aphrodite for 15 years, and in order to be true to this patron, she has never invoked a wealth god. When she asked me how she should work wealth magic, I told her to ask Aphrodite. Sure enough, Aphrodite used her wiles and influence to create a lot of wealth in this person's life, landing her her first six-figure position. Sometimes you may need to go to a wealth being or love being for help when you need it, but give your long-term contacts a try first. They may surprise you.

3. **Maintain sovereignty.** Your life is yours to live. Do not turn responsibility or decision-making over to angels, spirits, demons, deities, or anything else. Many people have a tendency to do whatever a spirit tells them to do, and it's a growing trend that needs to stop. Yes, it is traditional in many cultures, but not everything traditional is a good idea. The spirits do not live here and do not know all the nuances of how you want your life to run—that's your job. Evaluate nonhuman advice the same way you would evaluate human advice. By all means develop relationships, praise and worship, and make offerings. If, however, a god tells you to make an offering that will bankrupt you, I would recommend rethinking that relationship. Maintain your sovereignty.

x x x

Before we move on to the work, there is just one more being we need to cover in the next chapter, the one whose emblem graces the cover of this book: Jupiter.

References and Resources

Vodou Money Magic: The Way to Prosperity Through the Blessings of the Lwa, by Kenaz Filan (Destiny Books, February 16, 2010). A wonderful book detailing how different Lwa, the mysteries of Vodou, act on different aspects of money magic. Specifically geared toward people who have not been initiated into Vodou.

Encyclopedia of Mystics, Saints, & Sages: A Guide to Asking for Protection, Wealth, Happiness, and Everything Else, by Judika Illes (HarperOne, October 11, 2011). Excellent survey of saints and spirits that may be invoked in financial sorcery. Much deeper and denser with information than your typical encyclopedia of spirits.

Chapter 5

BY JOVE!

In the previous chapter I made the case that Jupiter is not the only planet you should turn to when working financial sorcery. Nonetheless, Jupiter is an immensely important power in financial work—so much so that this chapter is focused specifically on Jupiter and an arcana of magic that comes from him.

Sovereignty

Jupiter is not only the planet of wealth, accretion, prosperity, and wellness, but it is also the planet associated with sovereignty and the arts of kingship. When you boil it down, the goal of the financial sorcerer is to become the king of his domain, the sovereign ruler of his own financial fate.

The word sovereignty dates from the 14th-century Old French word soverain, which in turn is believed to be derived from the Vulgar Latin superanus, meaning "one who is over or above." The Merriam-Webster dictionary defines it this way:

1: supreme excellence or an example of it;

2 a: supreme power especially over a body politic; or

   b: freedom from external control.

The idea of sovereignty, then, is tied to the concepts of freedom and mastery.

Outwardly this is freedom from being ruled by others, and mastery of those parts of our world that we are responsible for: everything from actual property we own to deeds we perform. Inwardly this is freedom from being ruled by our own self-defeating habitual tendencies and mastery of our own wills. Secretly this is freedom from anything that obscures our true awareness and mastery of all that appears within its scope. The true financial sorcerer knows how to balance all of these aspects, and knows that none is more important than the other.

Those who seek only temporal power are hardly sovereigns or sorcerers. If money is the only thing you seek, becoming a banker or entrepreneur is a surer and more profitable path than magic. If power is what you seek, becoming a politician is a superior path to walk than sorcery. For the sorcerer there is no amount of money that is worth the wisdom of truth.

Those who seek only the rapture of divine union and quiescence of the mystic state are likewise not on our path. Such navel gazers lose the script for why they are even incarnated in the first place. To the sorcerer there is not much point in moments of primordial awareness if it does not carry over into the living levels of consciousness; no purpose to receiving the uncreated and clear light, if one cannot reflect it outward through world and deed; and no purpose in being a sovereign if you cannot leave the kingdom better than you found it.

For this reason, Jupiter, or Jove, embodies the type of being that the financial sorcerer hopes to become. It is for this reason that the planet Jupiter is most often associated with the supreme deity, or at least the most powerful deity of a pantheon, such as Zeus, Enlil, Dagda, Perun, Marduk, and, of course, Jehova.

It is also for this reason that a specialized seal of Jupiter adorns this book. Jupiter's power is such that he shakes the very heavens, which is why Jupiterian invocations are associated with freak thunderstorms and lightning blasts. Go forth and invoke Jupiter into your life and learn to shake your own heavens!

Invocation to Jupiter

I received the seal of Jupiter that graces the cover of this book three years ago during an extended working in which I invoked the intelligence and spirit of each planet, and asked them to transmit a sigil to artist and seer Matthew Brownlee that would tap directly into the planetary essence, regardless of astrological aspect. These seals directly represent the movements of each planet. When I began this book, I invoked Jupiter and asked him to support the book and the activities of those who read it.

As part of my work with the Gentlemen for Jupiter, I put on a suit and tie, lift a glass of whiskey, and make a toast to Jupiter every Thursday at the appropriate planetary hour. After starting the book, I decided to write a specific invocation that I could share with my readers:

O Supreme Sovereign

O Gracious Governor

Whose laughter unleashes lightning and life itself!

Who bestows bounty both boundless and blessed!

To you, I raise this glass and toast HAIL JOVE!

Hail to you who actualizes affluence.

Hail to you who is merciful in magnanimity!

Enhance my empire,

Open opportunity,

Activate my angels,

Protect me from the profane,

Favor me with fortune,

And grant me your grace.

Hail Jove!

The Jove Chant

After this invocation is performed you can chant the phrase Iovis Optimus Maximus ("Jove most great and most powerful") over and over. As you do so, see the words circling your heart. As they spin they throw off bolts of lightning. Feel the powers of Jupiter build within you and around you like a whirlwind storm. This is a chant specifically to build power and the presence of Jupiterian grace. It is not something to be silently meditated upon, but a chanted in increasing volume.

The Four Goddesses

One evening a few weeks after writing the Jove invocation, after my toast invocation on the day and hour of Jupiter I had a strong vision:

Jupiter appeared in his traditional Roman form as a bearded man seated on a throne holding a lightning spear. I asked that he aid me in assisting others, and he silently stretched out his hand and gave me four coins. On each coin was a dif-ferent goddess. When I took the four coins I suddenly found myself on Jupiter's throne, as Jupiter, surrounded by the four goddesses at the cardinal points around me inside ritual gates, forming a mandala around me that was not unlike the planetary seal of Jupiter from Agrippa's Three Books of Occult Philosophy (right).

The goddesses presented themselves to me in turn, laid a wreath upon my head, and raised a glass of nectar to my lips. As each goddess laid her hands upon me I felt a rush of empowerment. With each sip of nectar I felt a power rise up through my central channel and envelop me in bliss.

The first goddess was Victoria—the embodiment of Victory and Triumph.

The second was Libertas—the embodiment of Liberty.

The third was Concordia—the embodiment of Harmony.

The fourth was Abundanta—the embodiment of Abundance and Prosperity.

After telling a friend about the vision, he confirmed for me that all four of these goddesses did in fact appear on Roman coins at one time or another.

The other striking thing about the vision is that the function of these four goddesses closely matches the four karma actions that one might find in a Tibetan mandala where a central figure is surrounded by four supreme sons or youthful dakinis that represent the four magical actions ('phrin-las bzhi) of the Tibetan Tantric systems. These are:

x Paushtika-karma, for increase or abundance, in our case represented by Abundantia

x Vashya-karma, or enchanting magic, represented here by Concordia

x Raudra-karma, or wrathful action, represented here by Victoria

x Shantika-karma, or pacifying action, which can be represented by Libertas (although it is not an exact match)

When you wish to invoke the extra powers of the goddesses you perform the invocation to Jupiter and add the following:

Jove, send me the graces of the Goddesses of the four gates.

Victoria, overcome my competition

and conquer my crossed conditions.

Libertas, grant me financial freedom

and free me from fear and force of habit.

Concordia, grant harmony and healing

and smooth interactions with those around me.

Abundantia, grant me prosperity

and the bounty of your cornucopia!

You four goddesses take your places!

Surround me with the splendor of Sovereignty

And pour upon me the nectar of your grace.

Timing

To perform the invocations you can time your rite to the day and hour of Jupiter. There are two ways of determining when this is. The first system, and the one that most people use, considers Thursday the day of Jupiter, as I have already mentioned. Determining the hour of Jupiter for any given day is trickier. For one thing, a planetary hour is not 60 minutes, unless it is on an equinox. To determine the length of the planetary hour, divide the time between sunrise and sunset by 12. Each segment is one "hour." The first hour of every day after sunrise is always the hour of the planet whose day it is; in other words, the first hour after sunrise on Thursday is the hour of Jupiter. You then follow the Chaldean order and repeat again and again; in this case it would run: Jupiter, Saturn, moon, Mercury, Venus, sun, Mars, Jupiter, Saturn, and so on. The night continues the cycle; only the length of the hour changes because the length of time between sunset and sunrise will be different. If all this seems too complicated for you, go online and Google "planetary hour calculator." Plug in your city and you are good to go!

The other system, extolled in the Book of Abramelin, an influential grimoire from the 14th century written by Abraham of Worms, considers any time that Jupiter is above the horizon to be the day of Jupiter, and any time that Jupiter is directly overhead to be the "hour" of Jupiter. This is the system I like best, and again, technology helps a great deal: If you have a smart phone, just download Google Sky and take a scan. Isn't technology wonderful?

Once you have the time and the seal, simply stare for a few moments at the seal. Reach mentally through the seal to the powers of Jupiter. The series of seals that this comes from were designed to be direct portals to the powers that bypass most of the other influences that one may encounter. Once you feel you have a lock on it, raise a glass of whiskey or the drink of your choice (not water!) to Jupiter and consume yourself with prayer and devotion as you invoke.

The Lightning Glyphs of Jupiter

After performing the preceding invocations several times I asked Jupiter to transmit further arcana to assist in people's financial work. I received the strong feeling that instead of working alone, I should again work with Matthew, the seer and artist who designed the aforementioned Jupiter seal.

I invoked Jupiter and asked him to transmit seals that would be of use in financial sorcery, specifically geared toward working in our modern age. What followed were 16 flashes of spirit. I felt them as lightning flashes, each with a specific purpose. As the meaning and purpose of each arose in my mindstream, the corresponding image arose in the mind of Mr. Brownlee. Throughout the course of the next few hours we recorded the 16 glyphs you see here.

Precisely how you use the glyphs is up to you. Although I give suggestions in the following section, you should not limit yourself. The only rules I would prescribe are to treat the glyphs, and any surface that you inscribe them on, as sacred. Treat them as living things.

For Drawing Money

This is the most basic level of money magic. If you need a specific sum of money, draw this sigil on a piece of paper and list the amount on the circle. Pray to Jupiter that he grant your request, and when he does, bury the sigil in your yard or in the wilderness somewhere near you. Be sure to thank Jove profusely and make his work known to others.

Apart from being the most basic, this is also the only glyph that did not appear in one continuous line.

For Entrepreneurial Work

The concerns of starting your own business are quite different from those of other types of work. Problems can be much more delicate. You can grow too fast for your model, and your home business can interrupt your day job. There are a lot of intricacies.

Consecrate the glyph, using the invocation given earlier in this chapter or another method of your choosing, and place it at the center of your business activity. It can be your store. It can be your home office. It can be an envelope where you keep your paperwork. Wherever it is placed, leave it there unless you need something specific. When you do pray to Jupiter, address your need to the seal.

For Holding on to Money

Money-drawing is great, but holding on to it is just as important. Inscribe this glyph on a three-pronged or two-pronged sassafras leaf. Keep it in your wallet with you to curb spending.

You can also inscribe it on the corner of every statement you get from your retirement fund to help guard against losses in your portfolio.

For Finding a Job

The job finder is like a waving flag that announces your need for a job. It not only attracts potential work, but also makes sure that it is the correct work for your life.

When looking for work, trace this sigil in the air and see it burning in blue flame. Pray to Jupiter and request that the sigil infuse your resumes, cover letters, and anything else you can think of. Carry the seal with you on job interviews and wherever you may be networking with people who might offer you employment.

For Steady Work

In this economy no one's job is completely safe. Inscribe and consecrate this glyph and keep it in your office, cubicle, or desk.

For Promotion

The upward thrust of the lines on this   glyph are meant to constantly help elevate you to newer and better positions, be it a traditional promotion at work, a bump in your normal asking price for freelance work, or a large, sudden jump in market share for your own business.

Inscribe it on a brass triangle and wear it around your neck when seeking a promotion.

For Financial Discipline

From cutting up your credit cards and killing debt to forcing yourself to invest that $1,000 a month into a Roth IRA, financial sorcery can take an enormous amount of willpower. When the money-holding glyph is not enough, this glyph of self-binding will probably do the trick.

Warning: this glyph operates by binding you to your plan by whatever means necessary. The more you resist, the worse it will be. If you resist the nagging feelings and mental reminders, events will transpire that will institute that discipline for you. It's hard to waste money shopping when you have a broken leg. Use with care.

For Sweetening Relations

Very often the thing that is needed to land a job, get a promotion, or just get some extra cash is not a working directed straight at that aim, but a working aimed at improving relations between people. From interacting with your difficult boss to arranging a merger, money is intimately connected with people.

For Dominating Relations

If sweetening is not enough, or simply not appropriate, this glyph will help you influence a person or situation more directly. Take a business card or a picture of your target and draw this glyph over it. As you do, consider that the zig-zag lines bind the limbs of your target and the swirl at the top casts your influence over the senses and speech. At night place the seal in a box with your commands written around the inside walls so that it completely surrounds the person you wish to influence.

Remember that no matter how strong the spell, magic is only one of many influences on any person.

For Legal Matters

Use this glyph to smooth out any kind of legal matters you come across in your work, such as gaining permits for your building, incorporating, giving depositions, and so on.

Inscribe this seal on a candle representing the judge. Use it along with the glyphs for sweetening or dominance as needed.

For Protection From the Law

You might be thinking that this glyph is for drug dealers, gangsters, or other flagrant criminals, but that is not who this glyph was made for. When you consider the amount of legal businesses that begin as black-market operations, it is easy to see how important a glyph like this can be.

Even major corporations sometimes have quasi-legal aspects to their operation—For example, I once worked for a large and legal VOIP company here in the states that may or may not have been operating in Pakistan against that country's telecomunications laws.

For Defeating Competition

It doesn't have to be ugly. It doesn't have to be vicious. Competition is just a reality of the world. In finance, if you extend a "harm none" attitude too far, you will get clobbered. Every promotion that you get is one that someone else doesn't. Every time you increase your business, someone else likely suffers.

This glyph can be used directly on specific competitors in a similar way to how you use the dominating glyph, or it can simply be used on yourself to drive off and defeat all competition in a general way.

For Viral Marketing

This glyph is all about creating buzz. It is also designed to work specifically in digital formats, affecting copies of anything on which it is placed.

Creating a master copy of a product (or resume) that is marked with this glyph will set incalculable numbers of wheels in motion. It can also be combined with other glyphs in order to fine-tune the message. This is the first glyph of this set that I ever employed personally, and I can attest to its potency and speed.

For Intelligence Gathering

This is the information age. Whether you are looking for information about an investment, trying to anticipate sales, or trading in information itself, this sigil goes out into the world and helps bring the right info back to you.

This sigil seems to work best when visualized and released rather than inscribed on a substance.

For Reversing Bad Luck

In every disaster there is opportunity. In every misfortune, there is a fortune to be made. This glyph does not just help make the most out of a bad situation; it flips that situation around and spanks its bottom!

Lost your house? Time to blow through your debt while you live at your parents' house rent-free!

Stock market crash? That's just a sale on investments!

Job crisis? Time to start a resume-writing business!

Foreclosure crisis? Someone has to serve papers and care for the properties.

It is not always pretty, but this sigil will help you find the opportunity that you have been missing, amidst the disaster that just happened.

For Pure Luck

This seal is for when you need the universe to smile upon you. Inscribe this seal in gold ink on a piece of white card and keep it over your heart.

Do not be greedy or tempted to use it all the time. The more you use it the less powerful it will be for you. Keep it for special occasions when either certain things need to happen just right in order for you to succeed, or you just have no idea what the next move is and you need a little luck.

References and Resources

Planetary Hour Calculator: www.astrology.com.tr/ planetary-hours.asp. Website for calculating planetary hours. Just put in your location and it will give you the correct time.

Google Sky: www.google.com/sky/. Google sky is an android app that will show you where all planets and stars are in relation to your location. If you want to work with Jupiter right overhead, this is the app that will tell you when that occurs.

Chapter 6

THE SET POINT

In 1982 Dr. William Bennett and Joel Gurin were looking for an explanation as to why repeated dieting is unsuccessful in producing long-term change in body weight or shape. What they came up with is called "set point theory."According to this theory, there is a control system built into every person dictating how much fat he or she should carry—a kind of thermostat for body fat. Some individuals have a high setting, whereas others have a low one. Whatever attempts at dieting are made will revolve around the gravity of this set point.

Though Bennett and Gurin were speaking about a physiological process related to weight, psychologically speaking, we have all have set points relating to a wide range of things. For instance, most of us have a surprisingly firm set point regarding our station in life. We get programmed to expect certain things and no matter what we say we want, we tend to gravitate to those expectations. This field of gravity is more difficult to escape than you might think. No matter what we may want, somewhere deep in the mind is a nagging thought of what we are "supposed to have" or what we "deserve."

When you realize the truth of this and take a look at your own set points, you realize that the power of these points is immense. If we do not work directly on these set points, their gravity will keep all our sorcery circling in tight orbits around them.

Let's take a look at set points in various areas and how they can hold us back or propel us forward through life.

Wealth

We all say that we want to be wealthy, but that is just at the surface level of conscious thought. The subconscious mind tends to have a lot more sway in these matters and, unfortunately, no matter what you say you want, this part of the mind usually has a different idea of what you should have.

Nowhere is the action of the set point more visible than in high school. For many of us, other than the occasional present-day trip to the DMV, high school was the last place where we were exposed, day in and day out, to a cross-section of society.

Remember the kids from rich families who lived in the houses up on the hill, and whose parents were all doctors, lawyers, or bankers? Even if in college they thought they might like to be artists, chances are their set point overtook them and they gravitated toward being doctors, lawyers, or bankers. They accumulate assets just as their parents did, save and invest similarly to the way their parents did, and are generally progressing down the same road.

Down a societal notch are the middle-class students from average suburban homes. Their parents were white-collar workers with mid-level jobs, or were perhaps even small-business owners. Chances are that those kids make the same, or even a little less than their parents did because of the poor economy. The lure of comfort and the illusion of security helped reinforce their set point. For the most part, no matter what they say they aspire to, what they actually aspire to is the same level of suburban comfort and security their parents have. They avoid most financial risks and thus reap no rewards thereof. If they lose a job and fall beneath the level of comfort, they work hard to get back to it, but once they get back to the level of equilibrium they are comfortable with, they more or less just work to keep the status quo.

There are also the middle-class, blue-collar families. These kids maybe went to vocational school and became electricians, plumbers, or mechanics. On one hand they will talk about the desire for wealth just as often as anyone else. On the other hand they take extreme pride in being "blue collar," and in some cases take pride in their lack of education, which some see as elitist. You see this play out in modern politics again and again, especially on the right. The Ivy League grad with advanced degrees is seen as being out of touch with reality, and the less-educated person is seen as being a better candidate because he or she is "someone you can have a beer with."

At the lower economic strata are the kids whose parents just did not give a crap or were overtaken by problems such as alcoholism, drug abuse, or simply terrible poverty. Sadly, there are entire school districts where this is the norm, and a child in this situation may never even come into contact with a friend from an upper economic stratum. Although there are plenty of examples of people who have risen above their situation, more often than not people don't. Here too there is a certain pride that can manifest either positively or negatively.

On the positive side, pride can reinforce the idea that no matter where you are from there is beauty to your culture, good things happen, and all people have worth. For many it can be this pride that forces you to move your set point, and fire up the determination to manifest better things for yourself and your family. This is why some parents will sacrifice and save and go to extreme measures just to move out of a bad neighborhood. Even if they never got an education or a high-paying job, they know that just being raised among others who have that as an expectation will be good for their kids and will move their set point beyond what it otherwise would be.

On the other side pride can manifest negatively. I know kids from inner city schools who were beaten up for "talking white," and kids from poor white neighborhoods who were beaten for doing their homework and trying to be a college boy. In this case, pride in one's culture manifests as reinforcing poverty and punishing education.

Of course this mistrust of education and status doesn't only exist in America. I remember being at a restaurant in Kathmandu and talking to a friend about a recent scandal with the king of Nepal. The waiter overheard us and reminded us that "We Nepalese love our king. Only the educated don't like the king."

In all these cases, sociological and psychological factors impact the set point and set a baseline where you will more or less emotionally feel that everything is okay financially. For most of us, if we are in debt or lose a job, we work night and day to better our situation and get back to where our set point says we should be. If, however, we are making the average wage for someone in our peer group, but would like to be earning 6 or 7 figures, we tend not to work all that hard at it and leave our dreams as dreams. That is the power of the set point.

If you show an investment to someone from a wealthy background, they will take a look at it and see how they might make money with it because that is what their set point tells them is possible. If you show the same investment to someone from the middle-class, white-collar group, they will see all the ways that they might lose money with it because that is what their set point tells them to expect.

This may seem obvious to some of you, but you should spend some time mapping your set points so that you can eventually move past them.

The set point exists for other things as well.

Health

My parents and grandparents are all overweight. Not terribly over-weight, but enough that it is not healthy. Where am I? Surprise! I am also overweight. I am thin enough to go to the gym, run around with the kids, ride a bike for a few miles, and swim a few laps, but I carry enough extra baggage that I get winded faster than I would like, suffer from occasional acid reflux, and am putting myself at risk for heart disease and all kinds of other problems. I have been between 40 and 80 pounds overweight since I was about 23.

I would like to be back to my ideal weight, but my set point is comfortable being overweight, so weight loss doesn't get prioritized. Sad but true. At the beginning of the year I started a project to lose the weight, and I lost 25 pounds pretty quickly. That put me right at the outer rim of my set point's field of gravity, at which point I became complacent and yielded to temptation more often, prioritized other workings, and so on, and so on. As soon as time allows, I will begin to move my weight set point using the same methods that I used to move my wealth set point—the same methods that I will be teaching you at the end of this lesson.

Love

Ever hear someone say, "She's out of my league"? She wasn't. He just thought she was because his set point was dictating what he thought he could and couldn't attain. Ever see Dennis and Elizabeth Kucinich? That, my friends, is a man who did not let his set point dictate what was possible. Of course it works both ways: Men or women who know that they are a 10 in the looks department may not allow themselves to date someone who isn't, even though they secretly find the person attractive.

Other than looks, though, our set point can still make us think that someone is too good for us. We get into a good relationship, but we sabotage it because we are just waiting for our partner to realize that we do not deserve him or her. You may say you want a partner who puts you on a pedestal, yet find yourself always with a controlling and abusive person. Again, there is a disconnect between what you want and what your set point is.

Spirituality

There is a story about the great Tibetan Master Milarepa being questioned by his students about his former lives. Milarepa was known to manifest many different magical powers that defied explanation. Because of his magical and spiritual attainments, his students figured that he must have been someone important in a previous life. They insisted he tell them what Siddha or powerful Buddha he was in his past lives, or what Yidam or spiritual power he was an emanation of. Milarepa scolded them for not having faith in the path, for if they did, they would realize that you do not have to be someone special from birth; anyone who followed the path could attain Buddhahood in this very life.

Milarepa's students had a set point that told them that only very special people marked at birth could attain high spiritual states. Some of us have the same attitude. It is true that we are all gifted differently and that some people have natural advantages, maybe from past lives, family lineage or a special environment, but these only get you so far. I know a few very important and famous tulkus (reincarnations) who honestly are not spiritually fit to shine the shoes of other lamas who have no special birth and were raised in American suburbs.

The message is this: You can attain any level of wealth, health, love, or spirituality that you aspire to. It just takes work and a little adjustment of expectation.

Moving Your Set Point

There are many different ways you can move your set point, including pure force of will. Following is a method that I have found particularly effective, and with which my students have reported success.

Step 1: Releasing the Point

Your set point is largely the work of your past: how you were raised, your genetics, the neighborhood you grew up in, the school you went to, the friends you kept, the college you went to, the people you dated, the food you ate growing up, and so on and so forth. At a deep level, almost every action and reaction that you have is the result of patterning that stems from this list. The work of escaping these patterns entirely and living solely according to our own naked, un-patterned awareness is the work of enlightenment itself.

At the moment, we are only concerned with breaking free from negative patterns and self-sabotaging actions so we can move our set points. Begin by looking back at the past—not for what you think may be the causes of your set point, but for examples of you giving in to your set point. The time you were going to buy that rental property but chickened out. The time when you were considering getting an advanced degree but backed out because it seemed like too much work. The time when you were going to go for a promotion at work but did it halfheartedly, thinking that it really did not matter all that much. Think of any situation in which you chose comfort over progress.

These events happen to all of us. You should come up with at least three and as many as nine examples of real-life regrets. Once you have your list, perform the following ritual.

Perform a zone rite of your choice. This can be an LBRP, circle casting, or any kind of ritual that sets up sacred space.

Within that space perform the pillars and spheres exercise from Chapter 3 and imagine a blazing fire in front of you. This fire burns with such intensity that when something is consumed by it, not even the name of the thing remains.

Call to mind an image of the first event on your list. You should see it clearly in your mind, but because of your meditation, you should feel somewhat more distant and dispassionate about it. When you are ready, fold that image mentally into a cube and cast it into the fire. As you do so, say something along the lines of:

I release myself from the bondage of the past.

I cast my failure and my feelings about that failure into the razor fire.

In the space of spontaneous awareness not even name of obstruction exists.

PHET![1]

Repeat this process for everything on your list.

When you are done, you should again quickly perform the pillars and spheres ritual to rebalance the elements within the body.

Lastly, turn your attention upward through the central channel to the Star Center above the body, which is like a chakra that is located above the crown center and above the physical head. Sound this syllable:

HUE

It is pronounced just like the word hue but stretched out over several seconds.

Feel the energy of this center, which is connected to all stars everywhere, unlock and descend through the body, sealing the work done.

This syllable is part of a system of syllables for what I call "Facets of the Flow." In this case the syllable represents the primordial flow of spirit's constant descent into matter, which is relevant here because we are filling the energetic void left by our releasing of the past.

You should perform this ritual for nine consecutive days. You may feel very free after the first performance, but that is just the beginner's high. These are very difficult psychic programs to remove, and one session will never cut it. It may bring you into a mind state where you think you have got it, but it will not bring you to the next stage unless you have made it concrete through repeated performance followed and reinforced by real-life actions.

Step 2: Moving the Point

We have dealt with the past; now we must deal with the present. I am not going to suggest a ritual here because once you release your past and decide to move the set point, the only thing that really can move it is an all-consuming passion for attainment. You can work this into a ritual of your own design, but it is vital that that ritual only be part of an overall working that interpenetrates all parts of your life.

It has been said that we are what we think about all day, and your task here is to build a natural resonance between your current self and the self that you wish to be. Your actions can and should include the following four things.

Role model study: When Neil Strauss wanted to become the world's best pickup artist, he shut himself up in his house so that he could read the biographies of famous ladies' men, watch movies of the all-time greatest leading men, listen to tapes of people who had gone where he was headed, and generally immerse himself in models from which he could draw. In our case there are numerous biographies and collections of wisdom from the financially skilled. Read a book by Warren Buffet or Bill Gates. You can and should read a few books about personal finance, but the goal here is to immerse yourself in the wisdom of people who do it, and do it well—not necessarily those who are writing books about how to get rich.

Surround yourself with those who already have their set points on target: Many magic traditions utilize vows not to surround yourself with heretics and disbelievers. The usefulness of this has nothing to do thinking that heretics are evil, but the simple truth that the people you hang out with rub off on you. If you want to be a

Buddha, it works against your goal to surround yourself with people who do not believe in Buddhism or think that spirituality is dumb.

You may think it's callous to find friends based upon things like money, love, attraction, and the like, but the simple truth is that if you want to get rich, you should try to develop friendships with people who actually are rich. Not to ask them for money, mind you, but just to learn some of the things they know about it, and to have people to talk with. If you tell your poor friends that you are buying a rental property near the beach, they will tell you all the reasons that you will lose your shirt and how people never get rich from "schemes." If you tell your rich friends that you are buying a rental property, they will ask you about whether you are using the right tax loophole, what property manager you are using, and other things to make sure that you do not lose your shirt.

When I tell friends who are overweight that I want to lose weight, they share all the times they tried and failed, and then make sure to ask me out for a burger. My changing is actually a threat to their comfort with being overweight. When I tell the same thing to healthy friends, they ask questions about my diet and make sure that I am getting good advice about nutrition and overall well-being.

I am not advising you to abandon old friends, but just to find some new ones to add to the mix. It's not that your other friends are not being true; they just lack the knowledge and perspective to do anything different.

Thought management: Spend time every morning projecting your success, every afternoon killing excuses, and every evening replaying the day in a better light.

Hypnosis: Hypnosis is a powerful tool for moving self-perspective and releasing habits. I do recommend self-hypnosis, but only after an initial session with a hypnotist. I use some hypnotic methods in my work, but because I am not a licensed hypnotist, I have chosen not to share them. There is plenty of material out there and I urge you to investigate it for yourself.

Step 3: Re-Setting the Point

Again, no ritual alone is going to do this. No spirit is going to make this happen. Rituals and spirits may put you into a mind state that is helpful, but it takes your hard work to actually reach the stage that you want. Magical workings can be part of this process, but always remember: "First comes the working, then comes the work."

So what actually does the trick? Success does. You must go out and apply all the knowledge and perspective that you gained in the last step. You must go out and apply it...and fail. Then you must go out again and again until you succeed. There is no other way to do this. People claim that there is, but there isn't.

Read the remaining chapters in this book and apply them according to your needs. Get out of debt, find a better job, get promoted, start a business, invest, purchase assets. Success is the only way to re-set the point.

The moment that you start getting results, your set point will be re-set. You will no longer look at a job as the only way to make money. You will no longer think that you are just "supposed to" be making $30,000–60,000 a year. You will have released yourself from the past, learned the necessary skills, shifted the necessary perspectives, and actually succeeded in the first step of your new venture. You will not have to believe you can—you will know.

Chapter 7

DEBT-KILLING STRATEGIES

Now that we have talked about basic skills and learned to move our set point, it is time to get down to laying out the strategies we will use for making change in our lives. It's important to realize that different readers will be at different points along the financial spectrum: A reader who is very well off may not need to worry about radical debt strategies; similarly, a person who is on the verge of bankruptcy and having trouble keeping a roof over his or her head should not yet be thinking about long-term investments and acquiring assets. But no matter what your personal situation, I urge you to read through each section so that you can grasp the strategies and get a feel for how the sorcery hinges upon them.

Let's start from the ground up and assume that you, the reader, are exactly where a large percent of Americans are right now: deep in debt.

If some of the following material seems obvious to you, I commend you on your financial prowess. I only ask that you suffer through it because I know from feedback from students that a lot of people do not know these things and are in desperate need of this type of strategy. And even when you know the basics of a principle, it sometimes helps to have it all spelled out. The world changes radically and today's real estate mogul could easily be tomorrows pizza delivery guy.

The Debt Prison

Debt makes all the difference in financial health. Even if you earn income at just a hair above the poverty line, you can still build real wealth if you manage to live without debt. Conversely, it is also possible to have an income in the millions and lose it all in a flash if you are living beyond your means. It all comes down to those two piles of money I talked about in The Sorcerer's Secrets: The one coming in has to be bigger than the one going out, or, eventually, no matter how tricky your math, you will be screwed. Duh.

Unfortunately, it seems that this simple lesson is lost on more of us than not. Annie Leibovitz, MC Hammer, Nicholas Cage, Ed McMahon, Don Johnson, and Charlie Sheen are all on the list of rich and famous people who lost everything because they had more debt than income. I myself have been in debt, and I am willing to bet that some of you are carrying more than a healthy amount of debt as well.

Thankfully, sorcery can help, especially if we have a strategy. I break it down into eight steps.

Step 1: Assess Where You Are

Before we can do anything to advance ourselves from our current position, we have to know where we are. In other strategies I treat this more or less as a given, but not in debt magic. Debt is usually created and perpetuated by people who haven't a clue about where they are. I have never met anyone in significant and long-term debt who had a clear picture of what they earned or what they spent. Not one. That includes me when I had those issues myself.

I am going to speak frankly here: In most cases the ignorance is purposeful. People in debt are not stupid. People in debt are overwhelmed. Bills remain unopened because you know you can't pay them and looking at the actual number is just too depressing. Bank accounts get overdrawn regularly because actually looking at the balance before using the debit card can be just as bad. Taxes, utility bills, and credit cards are all subjects too daunting to deal with today, so you tell yourself you will cope with it another day. Today you will ignore the calls and leave the enveloped unopened. The day you actually deal with it, of course, never comes.

If this person I am describing is you, I want today to be the day that you deal with it. Today you are going to suck it up and deal. This very night I want you to open your bills, look at your paychecks, and gather as much info as you possibly can about the money you have going out and the money you have coming in. Get a real idea of where your money goes.

Start with the monthly bills that should be easy to look up. This includes:

x Mortgage/rent
x Car loan
x Other loans
x Credit cards
x Insurance
x Electricity
x Gas
x Water/sewage
x Trash collection
x Telephones (all of them)

- x Internet
- x Cable

After you get all this together, examine how much you spend on incidentals in the next few days. Keep every receipt for things such as:

- x Gasoline
- x Groceries
- x Eating out
- x Coffee
- x Dry cleaning
- x Gym membership
- x Vacation
- x Clothes
- x Entertainment of any kind
- x Personal care and grooming
- x Vices
- x Charity
- x Pet care
- x Magic books and supplies

Now it's time to measure this against the money you earn. First take a look at what you have:

- x Cash in your wallet
- x Checking account
- x Savings account
- x Money owed to you
- x Stocks/bonds

Then look at income:

- x Paycheck
- x Assets (yields on investments, payments from businesses owned, etc.)

If you are like most people, you will be surprised by the numbers—especially those going out. Even if you are not in debt, this exercise is worth doing every now and then. I am not in any particularly drastic debt at the moment, but I figured I would check out how much I spend at Starbucks: about $150 a month, or $1,800 a year. I am okay with that for now; I make enough to indulge myself. If I were deep in debt, however, that would be one of the first things cut out. As it is, the realization made me take the time to get a Starbucks gold card so that at least I get a free drink every few weeks.

Step 2: Macro-Enchantment

Now that you know where you are and where you need to be, you can perform your macro-enchantment to help you get there. A macro-enchantment is an overall spell or ritual that is done simply to get what you want—in this case, to be debt free. This is in contrast to micro-enchantment, which we will talk about shortly. Macro-enchantment is the only type of magic that most people do: one spell to achieve an end. It can take many forms; appeals to saints, gods, and other figures are popular. Invocations of the Holy Guardian Angel (HGA) or personal Genius are particularly effective in this type of work. Candle magic spells, evocations, and even mojo bags and talismans can help anchor a ritual.

Whatever it is that you are doing for your ritual, I strongly recommend picking something that is short enough that you can make a daily practice out of it, so that it reinforces your daily efforts. One simple prayer made popular by Bruce Wilkinson is the Prayer of Jabez.

The prayer is simple:

Oh that Thou wouldst bless me indeed, and enlarge my coast, and that thine hand might be with me, and that Thou wouldst keep me from evil, that it may not grieve me!

You could even change the word evil to debt. This simple prayer is so potent because it takes divinity and places it squarely in the center of our material lives—precisely what strategic sorcery is all about.

Step 3: Instituting Discipline

With your macro-enchantment taken care of, now it's time to focus on developing the discipline you have been lacking. You will need to constantly remind yourself to act according to your will and not your whim. Specifically, you need to stop bleeding money. To do this you need to take a hard look at the assessment you did and isolate expenses for shelter and food. Unless you are moving, your shelter should be easy enough to figure: It costs what it costs. Some of you may be in situations in which you bought more house than you could afford and there is no way you can continue on. In those cases you will need to explore your options for moving to a new living situation. Otherwise I just set that money aside every month and move on.

Food is another matter. If you have been eating out a lot, it's time to eat in. If you have been eating in, but spending as much as you would eating out (or more), it's time to learn to spend frugally. This might be a great thing for your body: an opportunity to cut out fatty foods and greasy snacks and such. Sadly, some people do the opposite to save money: Substances that pass for food on value menus at fast-food chains can seem like the most economic option, but they're not. If you are going to solve your problems you will need to be healthy.

Other people eat on the other end of the spectrum, doing their food shopping at Whole Foods and artisanal farmer's markets. Unfortunately, as the Michael Pollans and Alice Waterses of the world increase awareness of such fare, the prices keep going up and up, meaning that eating local and organic artisanal foods is increasingly an option of the rich—which, if you are in debt, isn't you. I am not suggesting that you eat junk, only that you find things at a regular food store that are relatively healthy and save the $9 Whole Foods salsa and $5 loaf of organic cinnamon bread from the farmers market for when you get out of debt. As inspiration I often think of Evan Lansing, a blogger who lived for a month on just $30. If he can do that, you can at least manage to cut your food budget in half for as long it takes to make a dent in your debt.

Other than these necessities, you need to figure out the bare minimum that you can live on, and then really live on it. Get inventive about it and challenge yourself. Figure out what gives you the best bang for the buck.

Do not just make the mistake of cutting everything you possibly can, though, because you will not be able to sustain it. Instead, look for the things that give significant enjoyment for relatively small amounts of money. Strangely, some books identify computers and Internet access as expenses to cut, but that just shows the age of the person writing. In reality, your computer and Internet connection probably provide you the biggest possible entertainment bang for your buck. In fact, if you are using your computer wisely you can get rid of the television, newspaper, books, and even house phones. If you went out and bought the best PC you could afford, supplemented it with a high-speed Internet connection, and then cut all the services and products that you could get via the Internet instead, you would probably save money month to month.

Here are a few Do's and Don'ts.

x **DO** go to the library and check out books.

x **DO NOT** buy more books. (I am aware of how hypocritical this is in a book that you probably purchased.)

x **DO** work out at home or outside, even if you have to buy some cheap weights to do it.

x **DO NOT** join a gym. If you belong to one, cancel ASAP. It's a money suck.

x **DO** invite people over and entertain with pot lucks and parties.

x **DO NOT** go out to dinners with friends more than once a month.

x **DO** join Netflix or another similar service if you like movies.

x **DO NOT** purchase DVDs or Blu-Rays.

x DO purchase yourself something new that you really want once a month as a treat.

x DO NOT buy many small things that are on sale because you are "saving money by buying it on sale."

In the past when I have suggested these things to people, they have always balked, as if following these guidelines would ruin their lives. If you are thinking along similar lines, there are three important things to keep in mind:

1. These are not permanent changes. They are changes to make until you are out of debt, at which point you may go ahead and reintroduce some luxuries.

2. You will find that your enjoyment of life doesn't hinge as much on anything outside of yourself as you thought it did. In the end you will be stronger and better in ways that have nothing to do with money. I guarantee it.

3. When you pay off a debt, it is like getting a raise. This very month I paid off cars that my wife and I purchased new. Suddenly we have 700 more dollars in the monthly budget, which is really nice.

Macro-enchantment is used for the overall effort of getting rid of debt; then, micro-enchantment is applied to individual steps in a strategy to ensure success. As for magical support for your discipline, make yourself a mojo bag for debt killing: High John for self-mastery, cinnamon for drawing money, and sassafras root or leaves for holding on to that money. You can embellish it as you will: slippery elm to aid in talking with creditors, cinnamon bark for bringing money, cascara and galangal for sorting out lawsuits, master of the woods for self-control. Use your imagination and ask for guidance.

Don't forget the Lightning Glyphs. Using the glyphs for financial discipline, reversing bad luck, and holding money can do wonders. You can visualize them in your aura, consecrate seals with them, or work them into a mojo bag.

Most important of all, meditate. You will constantly need to force your mind to recognize the whims of the moment as distractions from your true will. Sorcery will help in your efforts, but ultimately the efforts must be your own.

Step 4: Dealing With Credit Cards

This step may seem very similar to the previous one, but I separate this out as a step of its own because it presents some different challenges. I will be blunt: credit card companies are evil. They could hardly be more so if they were staffed by actual demons. In the old days you used to have to work up to getting a credit card. They would only give you a credit card if they thought that you would use it wisely and pay your bills. Somehow, in the early 1990s, the model changed. They figured out they made more from fees than from actual business, so they started giving cards away to anyone and everyone, specifically targeting people whom they knew would not or could not pay. This includes college students, the elderly, the poor, and people already in debt. In short, if you are using a shovel to dig yourself into a hole, a credit card company will be happy to give you a backhoe.

Most people who are in debt make their regular minimum credit card payments. Some people who are just starting to claw their way out of debt feel that this is what they should be doing: paying what the company says that they owe, even taking pride in being able to handle that. If you have a high balance and are in debt, you will never get out of debt by paying the minimum, and you will end up paying more in the end than you ever dreamed!

Let's say you have a balance of $5,000 with 17 percent interest. Your credit card minimums are typically 3 percent of your balance. Paying only the minimum every month, which is $150 for this month, it will take you 13 years and two months to pay it off! Worse than that, the final amount that you pay will be $9,031! You will pay an extra $4,031 on that $5,000 just for the pleasure of having Visa hold your debt for you.

If, however, you could squeeze $300 from your budget every month you can have it paid off in 20 months and pay only $700 in interest. Big difference, right? Then you are done. It's over. Best yet, once you are done, you can apply that $300 that you are already budgeting for to other debts, making even larger payments. This is how you work up to paying off the really big debts like student loans and mortgages.

If you have heavy credit card debt, go to an online credit card calculator and figure out how much you can pay and how long it will take. Then find a low-interest card to transfer the balance to and get it done. You can use these same calculators to figure out car payments and home mortgages. The same dynamics apply.

With all that said, I am not advocating your getting rid of your credit cards entirely. You need them for emergencies, for car rentals, and for a bunch of other activities. What I am advocating is that you stop using them for anything other than emergencies for now, and that you pay them off quickly. They are a necessary evil, but you should never forget that they are still an evil. It is easy to get right back into debt if you are not careful.

Step 5: Creditors

If you are deep enough in debt that you have stopped paying your bills and have people calling your house, this step is really very simple. After you have completed Step 1 through Step 3 you should have a good idea what shape your finances are in. All you need to do now is pick up the phone and talk to the creditors who are calling you.

One by one, talk to your callers and set up a plan that you can actually stick to. It's amazing how nice they can be when you make even the smallest effort. That goes for the IRS as well. I have had to deal with the IRS three times in my life: twice for me and once for my parents' business. Each time they were very understanding and easy to make a plan with. You tell them what you can do, and chances are they will agree to it.

Try to avoid third-party companies that make it seem as though they will do everything for you. Their ads suggest that they can reduce your debt to almost nothing, and when you are desperate and overwhelmed this can seem like a good idea. It is almost always not a good idea. They can rarely reduce your debt to less than you can on your own, and the fees that they charge will usually make up for the difference, leaving you just as stuck as before.

Micro-enchantments can be very important at this stage, and any type of influencing magic you know can be applied against your creditors. I recommend bringing their corporate logos to your money altar and placing them under the state or picture of  a great power. The seal of Saturn is excellent for this. If you are having a lot of trouble you can bind the paperwork up and place it in a master root. Another thing you can do is dress it with Bend Over oil and place the logo in your shoe so that you are stepping all over your creditors. Reading the influencing chapter of *The Sorcerer's Secrets* will give you a lot of ideas on how to employ conversational magic and more advanced influencing techniques.

If things are so bad that bankruptcy seems to be the only option, all I can tell you is to speak to a couple of lawyers. Don't take the step lightly; bankruptcy is not the panacea that it used to be. Thanks to the Bankruptcy Abuse Protection legislation from 2005, there is a lot that it won't cover anymore, and the damage it does to your credit is harder to repair than you think.

Step 6: Credit Reports

Now that you have handled the people who are knocking down your door, you need to check your credit report so that you can find out if you owe anybody anything else, and make sure that there are no companies reporting on you in error—which happens more often than you would think.

Put the stupid commercials out of your mind, though: You do not need to go to FreeCreditReport.com or some other outfit and pay them money. The AnnualCreditReport.com Website was set up to comply with the Fair and Accurate Credit Transactions (FACT) Act, legislation that requires the credit bureaus to provide consumers with a copy of their credit report once per year. It is the only official site where you can get a free copy of your credit report from the three major credit bureaus, Experian, TransUnion, and Equifax. Again, it's free once a year. Use it once a year. Find out if there are any mistakes, and if there are, contact the company and fix them.

Step 7: Spending Wisely

The last step of any debt strategy isn't about saving money, but about spending it. In the early stages of debt-killing you will not have a lot of money to play with. What you have must be spent judiciously. You will shop with a list and learn to stick to it. You will learn how to resist impulse purchases and notice how, a couple of hours or days later, you feel as though you didn't really need the item that badly after all.

As your debt starts to disappear you will have more and more money each week. The trick is not falling back into old habits. Continue to wait and evaluate whether you really want or need something. Think about the real pleasure it will give you and yours.

More than that, learn what money saved and invested can build up to. Things that you would ordinarily whip a credit card out for, like a computer or even a car, can be saved for and purchased without spending a nickel in interest more than you have to. Education and training also become possible when you have the ability to hold on to money and do something productive with it. The rest of the chapters in this book will help with this.

References and Resources

You're Broke Because You Want to Be: How to Stop Getting By and Start Getting Ahead, by Larry Winget (Gotham, December 27, 2007). Solid and simple book on digging your way out of debt.

Credit Card Calculator: www.creditcards.com/calculators/. This Website has a host of different calculators to help you get a handle on how and when you will have credit cards paid off. Knowing the reality is the first step to facing it.

Annual Credit Report: www.annualcreditreport.com. This is the official site for getting a free report from Equifax, TransUnion, and Experian once a year. Do not be fooled by imitators that ask you to pay money for the same service.

The Simple Dollar: http://thesimpledollar.com. Blog dedicated to simple financial wisdom that most people can follow. The blog specializes in ways to save money. Some are a little extreme, but all are worth a look.

Chapter 8

MANAGING MONEY

If you are in debt, the strategies in the previous chapter will help you get your life together. In the meantime (and even if you are not in debt), you need to think about how to optimize your financial life. If you are doing the minimum that most people do, chances are you have a checking account, a savings account, and a credit card. Your first step in exceptional financial sorcery should be to optimize these resources and set up permanent magical systems that will help keep wealth flowing smoothly in your direction.

Money Maintenance Magic

A staggering amount of magic throughout the world is aimed at maintaining a positive flow of wealth. Taking advantage of just a few of these, linking them to cunning use of accounts and credit, will give you a solid foundation upon which to build your future wealth.

Perhaps of all countries in the world, the one with the most prevalent and varied wealth magic is China. When you visit a Feng Shui supply store or even just a typical Chinese gift shop, you are presented with dozens of different good fortune charms and wealth-building fetishes. Whereas many religions ask you to look past worldly concerns and focus on the afterlife, Taoism very much values the life we lead right now and considers wealth and longevity signs of spiritual growth rather than detriments to the spirit.

My favorite piece of money magic from China is the Chan Chu, or Three-Legged Money Frog. The frog is seen sitting atop a bed of coins, and has a coin in its mouth. Very often it has stars on its back in the shape of the Big Dipper, an important constellation in Taoist magic: It is said to fill with chi from the void and pour down good fortune from the overflowing dipper. There is also usually a protective Pa Kua, an octagonal symbol containing the Yin Yang and eight Chinese trigrams (series of combinations of three lines) on the frog to protect the flow of money it brings in. You can purchase these almost anywhere that sells Chinese gifts, but they must be placed in the proper spot if they are to work correctly.

The best place is inside the front door of your home or the door to your office, facing inward. It should neither be on the ground nor too high; waist-level is perfect, as this is where most wallets are kept. Money frogs should not be kept in the kitchen or bathroom. Some people remove the coin from the frog's mouth at night and face him outward, but I do not. Instead, I leave the coin in, and if it falls out, I treat it like an early warning of things going wrong financially. This system has proven eerily accurate throughout the years.

Moving from China to Japan, another popular wealth talisman is the Maneki Neko, or Becoming Cat. This cat statue, usually ceramic, has one or both hands raised with palm outwards, which looks like a wave to most Americans, but in Japan is considered a gesture of beckoning. It is commonly thought that cats with the right paw raised are used to attract customers to a business and cats with the left palm raised are used to attract good fortune to a home. The cats are also popular among the Chinese and are sometimes mistaken as being Chinese in origin.

If you get the Feng Shui bug you will discover many practices that are said to help increase the flow of wealth, from very strategic positioning of items such as fountains and Pa Kua mirrors, to simple acts such as making sure all toilet bowl lids are closed when not in use, lest money escape down the plumbing.

Moving back to the West, an extremely popular method of enchantment is to use floor wash to occasionally cleanse one's house of negativity and invite wealth in. You can make this a two-day affair by cleansing your home on a Sunday or Tuesday (the days of the sun and Mars, which are good planets for cleansing and routing out negativity) with a spiritual-cleansing floor wash. There are many recipes for this, including lemongrass, pine, and ammonia, but you can also use a store-bought product like "Chinese Wash," which is designed for the same thing. You begin at the top floor and wash down to the bottom floor and out the door. The idea is that you are pushing out all negativity along with the wash. If you have carpets, you can use a spray bottle rather than a wash.

After you have cleansed the house, you can follow up on a Thursday or Wednesday (the days of Jupiter and Mercury, which are the best planets for drawing money and doing business) with a money-drawing wash—one that has cinnamon, sugar, and chamomile. You do this in reverse, starting outside the house and working your way inward and upward to draw in that positive influence. This is also an opportune time to beef up your protection spells (for example, your nine pieces of devil's shoe string in the walk, or the seals at the gates of your property). Protection and money-drawing go hand in hand if you want to protect your holdings.

One of my rituals with which a lot of people have had success is the cashbox. Find a cheap wooden box that is big enough to hold a good amount of papers and items. (It doesn't need to be huge; mine is 6 inches by 3 inches by 3 inches.) Carve, engrave, or paint the symbols of the planet, intelligence, and spirit of Jupiter on the front of the box. Put four Jupiterian astrological symbols on the lid along with one of the pentacles of Jupiter from the magical grimoire The Key of Solomon—the choice is yours. On the inside of the lid, place the Kamea (or "magic square") of Jupiter. Paint or stain the box an appropriate color, such as blue for Jupiter or gold for wealth. Rub the outside of the box with money-drawing oil and the inside of the box with money-keeping oil. Pay special attention to rubbing the oil into the symbols you carved or painted onto the box.

After you have constructed the box, go to the place where you do your banking and take a little dirt from the land just outside the bank. If you live in a city and there is no natural ground outside the bank, then you can take some dust from the bank or even some dirt from a potted plant. Line the bottom of the cashbox with the dirt. You can place other symbolic items in the box as well. In mine I have:

x A gator's hand for "grabbing" money and opportunity

x Sassafras leaves for holding on to the money I get

x A lodestone for attracting money

x Irish moss, allspice, cinnamon, and other money-drawing herbs and spices

Take some cash and place it in the box. Leave it there for a week. Then take it out, and "dress" each bill with Mercurial symbols: four on each side, making eight in total, the number of mercury. Spend the cash as you see fit. The idea here is that the cash is now a talisman and will attract more cash to you, which you then place in the box. If you do this correctly, you should soon be able to afford to put more cash into the box, thus increasing the amount that returns, just like any good investment.

Yet another popular spell (one that is at the center of my own financial altar) is the petition and lodestone spell. I actually like to do this petition on New Year's Day, but any day will do. To perform this spell, write out your financial wishes in a letter to the gods. Be specific about things that you would like to work on throughout the next year, and opportunities that you would like to open up. Write it all down and then fold it up and place it on a metal plate—preferably tin, the metal of Jupiter. If you want to decorate the petition with sigils and oils, feel free to do so.

Then take a lodestone, the largest you can find, and cleanse it with some whiskey to remove any psychic patterns from it. Place it on the petition and repeat the following prayer:

O thee powers of Earth.

Arise and take up residence within this stone.

As I fulfill you with offerings of iron

May you fulfill me with offerings of wealth.

Act according to the will and words that support you.

As I fulfill you, So you fulfill me.

So it is written, So it shall be.

Every week (or even every day, if you can keep up with it), you should sprinkle some iron grit on the stone. As the grits are attracted to the stone, the powers in the stone will attract the events and wishes expressed in the petition. As you make your offerings, utter a little prayer to keep it going.

At the end of the year, and every year after that, change the petition to accommodate changing circumstances. Bury your old petitions on your property to symbolize that their blessings are now part of your life. If the wishes in the petition change drastically—for instance, you decide you do not want something that you asked for in the petition, or you change your career direction—simply perform a small offering of thanks to the powers you have summoned into the stone. Clean it with whiskey and start again with a new petition.

There is really no end to the amount of spells you can set up to draw, hold, and protect money on an ongoing basis—everything from physical-based magic, as I've been describing, to very complex astral constructs that I don't have the room to explain in a book like this, but which can also be very effective. The effectiveness of simple prayer on a daily basis must also not be overlooked. The idea is that you should pick just a few of these rituals and keep up with them. Do not try to do everything under the sun or you will drive yourself crazy keeping up with magic that ultimately is not doing anything because other spells are already doing it.

If you really want to help make that magic more powerful, you need to apply your cunning to the places where you keep your money and to the systems you have in place for managing it.

Checking Accounts

Your checking account is your mercurial extension of financial magic—it's where the action happens. Whether or not you literally invoke Mercury or another power to help oversee the account is up to you. For the record, I don't invoke to oversee my accounts. Too much magic is overkill.

Whether officially empowered or not, you owe it to yourself and the spirit of Mercury to make sure the account is optimized. To start with, make sure you have no fees and no minimums associated with your checking account. If you do, ask them to be waived. If the bank won't do it, find a new bank. Make sure that you have good access to your money at all times: Some online checking accounts and credit unions may have excellent terms but can be a hassle when you need access to cash. Remember, this is Mercury—movement is key!

Also make sure that you do not have overdraft protection. Like many scams, this is a program that sounds as though it's there to protect you, but it's really there to take advantage of you. The idea of overdraft protection is that if you accidentally overdrew your account through using your debit card, then the bank would do you the favor of covering the charge in exchange for a small overdraft fee of $35 to $50. This happened to me once because of a simple mistake, and I got charged $40 for a cup of coffee, and then another $40 for a sandwich. That's an $80 lunch that should have cost $7!

Many banks enrolled people in this type of program automatically, but had to take their customers out of it in April of 2010 because of the new fairness laws passed by Congress. So now they are trying to get people to sign up for it on their own by presenting it as a service. They send you an e-mail after your debt card gets declined, offering this wonderful service. It is, however, still a scam. There are too many good banks out there to tolerate a bad one that is trying to scam the customer. Just because it's legal doesn't mean it's not a scam.

Savings Accounts

Some people think of their savings account as the main place to keep long-term savings, but it shouldn't be; they belong in IRAs and other types of investments that have better interest rates. We will talk more about these later.

Your savings account is first and foremost where you need to park about three months of living expenses in case of emergency. It is also where you want to put money you are saving for special purposes such as vacations, down payments, and large-ticket items that you are going to purchase within a few months to a few years from now.

Although I like using a brick-and-mortar bank for checking accounts, online savings accounts have consistently better interest rates than traditional banks. If you are going to put $10,000 somewhere, why not put it somewhere that it is going to earn 3 percent ($300 a year) rather than 0.5 percent interest ($50 a year)?

Whereas your checking account is Mercurial, your savings account is Jupiterian, and can be enchanted as such. Remember, this is not a single spell. It is a long-term working. This means you should not make any deals for extensive offerings on a daily or weekly basis unless you plan on following through. It is simple enough to just place your account balance sheets on your financial altar under a seal or statue of Jupiter and perform the invocation of Jupiter. I do mine the first Thursday of every month.

Credit Cards

I know I told you in the previous chapter that credit card companies are evil and out to get you. I still hold that is basically true, but unfortunately they are a necessary evil. Want to rent a car, take a cruise, or stay in a hotel? Unless you are willing to pay wads of cash as a security up front, or have money frozen in your checking account because you used a debit card, you need a credit card. Not a debit card that works as a Visa (for instance), but one that draws on your checking account. You need a real credit card. Just make sure that you optimize it.

Negotiate a low annual percentage rate (APR) on the card you have, or find a new card with a low APR. As I mentioned in the last lesson, when making minimum payments, the bulk of your payment goes toward interest, with very little going to principal. Even if you are not now in debt, you never know when financial situations may arise that will put you in a position such that you can only make minimum payments, and possibly even need to use your credit card for food and other essentials. Bad times happen to everyone, and when they do, the low APR will make a huge difference when you are recovering.

If you choose a card with rewards, make sure that they are rewards that you will use. For example, sometimes cards will extend the warrantee of electronics and other appliances beyond the factory warrantee, and travel cards often offer great rewards on flights and hotels as well as excellent terms. In fact, there are a lot of people financing free flights around the world by purchasing thousands of dollars a month in $1 coins from the government, and then using that same money to pay the credit-card bill at the end of the month! This tricky but legal maneuver gains people enough travel miles to fly just about anywhere for free.[1]

Another great thing about a quality credit card is concierge service, which provides people you can call to do just about anything that a concierge at a hotel would do: look up information, make reservations, find flights, book tickets, provide reviews, and so on. John Hargrave, author of Prank the Monkey, wrote an article about how far he could push his concierge service. He used it to find hard-to-get cheese, solve crossword puzzles, hook him up with a motivational e-mail service, research the waitlist and cost of private space travel, and all kinds of other things.[2]

Having a credit card is a necessity, but the only way to avoid the pitfalls is to pay your complete balance on time every month. Apart from that, there are two more rules I want you to remember.

1. Avoid the credit-card offers that come in the mail; they rarely have the best terms. Instead, do a little research and find a card on your own.

2. Do not open more credit cards than you need, especially retail cards. Never take advantage of the "extra 10% off" they offer you at the register for opening a store card. These cards have terrible terms and awful rates. You will pay more in the long run, trust me.

Building Your Credit Score

Your credit score and report affect many aspects of your life. For example, if you want a loan for a vehicle, a house, or a new business, it will be the single most important factor in determining your rate. Even employers are looking at credit scores as a condition of employment. If you are or have been in debt, you probably have a bad credit score.

In the last chapter I spoke about how to obtain your credit report and how to fix any errors on it or find unpaid debts that you did not know about. Now that you have paid off your debt—and not before—it is time to work on raising that number. The first step is knowing how the score is calculated, and how to affect each aspect of it. Here's a breakdown:

x   35% of your score: Payment history—Pay your bills on time.

x   30% of your score: Balance owed vs. available credit—Get your credit limit raised and keep your balances low. Once out of debt you should never carry a balance month to month on a card.

x   15% of your score: Length of credit history—If you don't have any bills to pay, get some. If you have a bad history, start making a good history. There's no fix for this but time.

x   10% of your score: Length of Credit accounts—Value your older accounts, as they show reliability.

x   10% of your score: Types of Credit—Having a credit card is good. Having a car payment is good. Having a house is good. Provided, of course, that you are actually keeping up with everything. Variety is key.

Work on it. It takes time. It's hard work but the rewards are many. With a good credit score you will get better mortgage rates, better credit card rates, better insurance premiums, and even possibly a better job. You actually save money by paying your bills on time and having a good score.

I have met people who have summoned spirits in an attempt to raise their credit score or get loans despite their credit score, but other than the occasional oversight from a banker, there is not a lot the spirits can do. Instead you should do magic that increases your discipline.

Taxes

Because this chapter deals with bank accounts, credit cards, credit scores, and other money management that just about everyone has to deal with, I thought I would end it with everyone's favorite topic: taxes.

In the previous chapter I spoke about the IRS being relatively easy to deal with if you just suck it up and work with them. That is true, but it is not a pleasant experience. My first and primary advice is this: Just pay your taxes.

The only reason that I am even mentioning taxes at all is that when people start getting clever at managing money, they can start to get too clever for their own good. One example of this is a piece of advice that I hear over and over again year after year, often from famous advisors. I hear it on NPR. I see it on CNBC. I read it on financial blogs. Worse yet, I even know two people who acted on this advice. It ended up costing them a lot of money.

The advice in question is about whether you should have the government withhold to ensure that you get a refund at the end of the year or have the government withhold the minimum possible—or even claim exempt—and pay them at the end of the year. The bad advice I always hear is this: Do not let the government hold on to your money all year and let them earn interest on it. If you hold on to it, you will earn the interest on it and end up paying the same amount of tax in the end.

The math is technically correct; if you just put the money in your savings account, you will earn interest on it all year, and then pay the government what you owe at tax time. So why do I think this is bad advice? Simple: You won't follow it.

You will have the government withhold the minimum, but during the year, 99.999999999 percent of you will not put that money into a savings account. You will spend it.

Think about it. You know I am right. Do you really want to keep track of your tax withholding yourself? How about the overall feeling at the end of the fiscal year: Do you want to get a nice fat direct deposit in your account, or do you want to write out a check to the IRS?

Now let's say that you do manage to execute this perfectly and have all the money set aside in April to pay the government. How much interest did you gain for your effort?

The average tax refund is $3,000. The interest from a typical savings account with $3000 in it at .75 percent is about $22.50 a month. My coffee costs more than that every morning.

So, you can spend a lot of time managing your withholding throughout the year, risk not having enough come tax time, and experience the downer that is writing a huge check to the government, all so that you bank a big $22.50 a month. Or you can have someone else take care of it and get a nice check at the end of the year. To me, it's a no-brainer.

Sometimes being a financial sorcerer means not taking the clever road and just doing what everyone else does.

References and Resources

Mint: https://mint.com. Online money management made simple and free. Coordinates accounts, investments, mortgages, and more. Makes budgeting easy by creating visual displays of your income and spending, and offers mobile apps. Excellent security.

Savings Accounts: www.savingsaccounts.com. Survey of what different accounts offer in terms of APY, fees, minimums, and so on.

How to Speak Money: The Language and Knowledge You Need Now, by Ali Veshi and Christine Romans (Wiley; November 8, 2011). Excellent tutorial on how money works in the modern day. Written for those new to the subject, this book will get you up and running on money management.

Chapter 9

JOB-FINDING MAGIC

Given the state of the economy it is a pretty sure bet that more than a few of you who read this book are currently out of work. You are, of course, not alone. On the cable talk shows and radio programs you constantly hear about the unemployment rate being higher than 10 percent. Here's the thing no one wants to talk about: the unemployment rate means almost nothing. At one point in 1982 the unemployment rate was almost 11 percent, but Reagan was re-elected and no one was as nearly as concerned as they are now. That is because what matters is the employment offering rate. As long as there are jobs for people to move into, the unemployment rate is not as important as people make it out to be. In other words, it's not how many people that are out of work that matter, it is how many jobs there are out there to be filled. Make sense?

Unfortunately, the employment offering rate is even worse than the unemployment rate. It's actually frightening. According to the Bureau of Labor Statistics, if we filled every open job in America right now, only one in five people currently collecting unemployment would have a job. As of this writing, in America it is pretty common for people to exhaust their 99 weeks of unemployment insurance without having found a job.

Those who do find work are finding that they are making less, and sometimes even just half of what they were making previously. Because there are so many people applying for every open position, companies can pick and choose who they want for any position. Jobs that formerly would offer a good living to people with a high school diploma now require a bachelor's degree. Entry-level positions that were formerly open to recent college grads now are asking for years of experience. The situation is grim.

But you are a sorcerer. A sorcerer can make opportunities out of lack of opportunity. The following sorcerous strategy has worked for me, and for many of my students as well.

Step 1: Macro-Enchantment

Macro-enchantment, as I have previously explained, is the large, overseeing operation you do to guide the overall project. So start out by doing a ritual aimed simply at finding work that is appropriate for you, brings in the money you need, and does not conflict with your spiritual/magical efforts. Exactly what form this working takes is up to you. You should rely upon your own intuition, divinations, and spiritual guides to decide. Whatever you do, your macro-enchantment should set up the overall quality of the work and attune you to powers that are genuinely spiritual as well as material.

After you do your macro-enchantment it is time to focus on the micro-enchantment.

Step 2: Putting the Word Out

People use an enormous amount of energy searching through job ads and Websites. That is good to do, but it is nowhere near as important as getting the word out to your personal network and contacts that you are looking for work. According to CollegeRecruiter.com, 80 percent of job openings are not listed anywhere at all and are instead filled by personal referral.

Some people find this idea off-putting, but it should be liberating: Rather than hundreds of applicants, there will be only a few. If you lack a degree but have the essential qualities and experience for the job, a personal connection will help you get that across to the company.

Putting the word out about being laid off should be your first and most vital step to finding new work. Obviously you will call your close friends and family, and perhaps use LinkedIn and Facebook to send the word out to your wider network. Take the time to look up prior coworkers and people you haven't spoken to in years.

As a magician there is a lot you can do to amplify and, importantly, refine this effort. Invoking the powers of Mercury is a good bet for this, as are the elemental powers of air. If you have been meditating regularly, you may have the clarity of mind to sense what my friend Persephone calls the philotic lines,[1] the psychic channels that exist between all people.

This is also an excellent time to employ the lightning glyphs for viral marketing, steady work, and job-finding together. Working these three together into a petition, charging it with an invocation, and carrying it with you can work wonders.

Step 3: The Custom Resume of Mercury

As of this writing, according to the bureau of labor statistics, for every professional job in America there is currently an average of 80 applicants. There are so many people applying that companies are using any methods they can to narrow down the number of interviewees. Unless you have a personal advocate in the company to speak for you, you need to have a plan that will get you noticed. You need to reduce yourself from being one in 80 to just being the one. Thankfully, even without magic you can reduce the odds against you just by taking some common-sense steps and doing the things that others don't.

The first step is simply making sure that your resume is tailor-made for the job you are applying for. There was a time when everyone would have one resume they would send out to all jobs—that time is long gone. Given the manner in which companies need to sort applicants just to get down to manageable levels, today's job seekers need to re-edit or even rewrite their resumes to reflect exactly what the ad or contact says the company is looking for. The resume should literally be a mirror of what the company is asking for in the advert.

Here's an example of why. If the ad says "a/r" experience and you write on your resume that you have "accounts receivable" experience, this simple change may get your resume tossed in the trash pile—even though a/r is short for accounts receivable! Why? Many times your resume is going to be scanned by computer to determine if it is a match for the advertisement. Even if it is a person going through the pile of 80 resumes it is certainly not the boss or even someone in the relevant department. It's the secretary. This person may not have any knowledge of the job whatsoever, and is just going through the applications getting rid of all the resumes that do not have what the ad asks for. They don't know that a/r means accounts receivable. All they know is that your resume doesn't say what the ad does, and that the others do.

The best resume advice I have ever gotten was to create a multi-page c.v. (which stands for curriculum vitae, Latin for "course of life") that contains a long, exhaustive list of every last thing you have ever done on any job. When applying for a job, go through this list and grab the relevant bits and place them in the resume, making sure to edit them to match the ad as closely as possible.

If you customize your resume for the job you are applying for (and of course have no mistakes or formatting errors), you just went from being one in 80 to one in 40.

I will talk about how to empower your resume with sorcery in a moment. First, though, I want to talk about the next step because these two go together.

Step 4: The Cover Letter of Venus

The next step is the cover letter. Think of your resume as your Mercurial talisman—it transmits information and tells them that you are qualified for the job. Your cover letter, then, is your Venus talisman—it tells them why they will fall in love with you when they meet you. The ideal cover letter takes an item or two from your resume and places it within a story. It shows you in action. Unless you are at the executive level, it should be short and to the point. By all means look at examples online, but for god's sake don't copy them. The employer will have gotten a dozen of those already.

Here's the great part: According to a friend of mine who is a hiring manager at an IT company, only 40 percent of applicants send out a cover letter. Although this is not a hard statistic, it does show a simple way to differentiate yourself. If you sent out a cover letter with your application you went from being one in 40 to one in 16. Not bad for just doing what everyone should be doing anyway. Better still, cover letters are the first place where you can not only list qualifications, but also make the argument about why you are right for the position at the company you are applying to.

Of course, we are sorcerers. When I spoke about the resume as Mercurial talisman and the cover letter as Venusian talisman I was not being figurative. You should actually charge them as talismans.

When loading physical objects with magic, a lot of people look to Hoodoo supplies to do the job. I have been witness to many conversations about how best to do this; what oils, inks, and powders would be best. These conversations always leave me shaking my head because they overlook two very obvious and important factors. The first question is: Are you applying for jobs at the mall in 1992? These days even retailers request that you submit your applications via computer. By all means bring a hard copy of your resume to your job interview, but in this day and age, the interviewer will already have it from the e-mail you sent.

Second, you should never ever do anything with magic that will work against you on the non-magical level. In this case, any perceptible weirdness on your resume will automatically disqualify you. Oil will make it look as though you just ate fried chicken and wiped your hands on the resume. Invisible ink will show up in certain lights, and those sigils you are drawing will definitely creep the hell out of some people. Powder is usable if you get it all off the resume, but the benefit is not worth the chance of making it look as though you are handing in a paper dusted with anthrax or cocaine. So if you want to avoid looking like a terrorist, a serial killer, or a slob, you should avoid the powders, invisible inks, and oils. Materia helps magic, but it is not necessary for magic. There are plenty of other ways to charge your documents.

First and foremost is a ritual reading of your resume and cover letter to charge the words themselves. You can call forth a spirit or even group of spirits and read it to them, asking them to empower your words and affect the minds of those that read them. Angels, incidentally, are ideal for this—they are messengers, after all.

The other option is to charge a master copy on your altar that you dress with all the incense, oils, and crazy sparkly sigils that you want, the idea being that what you do to that master copy affects all other copies, electronic and otherwise. If you can get links to the person you know will be reading the resume, you can create a honey jar or do some other type of working on your altar using the sweetening glyph.

Finally, if you simply must do something to the physical resume and cover letter that you are handing off, try passing it over a candle flame, tracing energy sigils in the astral, or anything else that does not require physically altering the resume. I am all for materia magica, but not when it will make your mundane efforts look sloppy.

If the custom resume and cover letter got you down from one in 80 to one in 16, effective sorcery will get you down to one in 8 or so. Enough to land you that interview.

Step 5: The Interview

At the interview you will use all the tricks of the trade, both magical and mundane. At the simplest level you should make sure that you are clean, smiling, charming, dressed for a job two steps above the one you are interviewing for, and have solid answers to common interview questions such as what your worst quality is. Too often in interviews applicants present themselves in overly personal terms and talk about what they are looking for from the company instead of talking about what they are bringing to the company. Ask about your role, ask about previous people in the position, ask about the team; be succinct, know why you are at the interview, and ask for the job.

As for magic, start with a talisman and an invocation. Keep it simple. In *The Sorcerer's Secrets* I wrote a chapter on influence magic that will give a good start to conversational sorcery and the types of magic you can employ during an interview. I am not going to cover them all here because this is one area where having only a little knowledge really is dangerous. If you know how to do it, by all means employ conversational sorcery, covert hypnosis, and any other tricks of the trade. Just go lightly with it. Looking as though you are trying to hypnotize the interviewer with googly-eyed staring or overemphasizing embedded commands will not land you the job. Unless you know how to use NLP (neurolinguistic programming) and conversational sorcery without looking like a creepy boob, avoid those methods.

There is, however, one thing that you must not avoid: the thank-you letter.

Step 6: The Thank-You Letter

Remember when I said only 40 percent of applicants send a cover letter? Well, according to the York Technical Institute only 4 percent of applicants send thank-you letters after interviews! If your interview was over the phone, an e-mail thank you is acceptable, but if they took the time to meet with you in person, you should drag your butt to the post office and mail the interviewer a proper thank-you card. Do it on the way home from the interview so it gets there ASAP. Doing so shows you have class and that you follow through on tasks. This one move alone can take you from being one in 20 to being just one. As with the documents discussed earlier, do not dress the thank-you with smelly or messy materia. Breathe a prayer onto it and let it go.

As for the letter itself, purchase a nice thank-you card that does not have a lot of frills or designs on it. If you there was something you did not mention in your interview, this is a chance to mention it as long as it remains short and simple.

Here's a little anecdote that shows how important the thank-you letter is. I know someone who was getting his wife a job at his company, and even though she got her interview through personal connections, the hiring manager mentioned to her husband that she must have forgotten a thank-you card, and that he doesn't hire people who don't send one.

Step 7: Negotiation

Entry-level jobs often do not have a negotiable salary, but most private industry jobs above that level do. Everything from software engineers to window treatment installers negotiate their salaries, and you should too.

Outside Europe and America people are used to negotiating a price for everything. If you walk into a shop in Nepal and pay the asking price for a T-shirt, you are probably paying 50 to 100 percent more than a tourist who knows how to negotiate. To these folks, negotiating is normal, but in Europe and America that is not the case, and many who could be getting paid more right out of the gate don't because they are uncomfortable negotiating salary. In bad economic times, people are even less likely to negotiate because they are afraid of negotiating themselves out of the job. This is an understandable fear, but not one you should give into. If you approach negotiations in a smart and friendly way, negotiating shows the company that you have pride, standards, and a sense of your value, which in turn usually leads other people to think you are valuable.

I have found that the best magic for this is not any kind of controlling or influencing magic, but rather a combination of sweetening Venusian magic between you and the company, and commanding magic applied to yourself.

In the first case I would recommend a simple honey jar. Take an extra business card from your interviewer and place it in a jar with your own card or a piece of paper with your name on it. Fill the jar with honey, molasses, sugar, and some licorice root and cinnamon sticks. Invoke whatever powers you like of a benevolent Venusian nature to sweeten the relations between you and the people hiring so that they look kindly on your suggestions and don't hold any missteps against you. If you can consecrate the jar at the day and hour of Venus, that is a bonus.

On the commanding end of things, you may simply anoint yourself with commanding oil (not too much) or carry a seal of Jupiter on your person. Other ideas are a mojo bag with a whole High John Root in it anointed (fed) with an appropriate oil that is not too smelly.

Most importantly, remember these rules for negotiating:

x Try not to talk about salary until the end of the process. It is not easy to find the right person for the job, and the more time you have to make the case that you are that person, the better your position will be for negotiating.

x If possible, let them name a number first. It may be higher than you expected. You can then accept it or tell them that you were thinking of a number slightly higher than that and see what they say.

x   Know the going rate for the position. Google is your friend, but so are colleagues in the same or similar positions at different companies. Having a group that you are not in direct competition with, but with whom you can discuss salary, is a great sort of financial coven to be in.

x   Sometimes a company cannot offer a salary above a certain limit, but can offer additional bonuses, options, or benefits. If you are hitting a wall with salary, try to feel out what the company can be flexible with. An extra week of paid vacation per year is nothing to sneeze at.

x   Keep it friendly. They are not the enemy. You are working together to arrive at a deal that you can both live with.

x   If you are paralyzed with fear about negotiating, go to a flea market or street fair and try to negotiate with vendors there. It is good practice, and will help you get your mind in gear to negotiate.

Altering the Strategy

You must also know that the strategy can be altered according to individual needs. For example, someone applying for a job at a convenience store will need different tactics than someone applying as the chief financial officer of a bank. Still, the basic tactics are the same. Use macro-enchantment to invoke guiding and overarching powers, and then use micro-enchantment to amplify your efforts at each stage in the process.

Of course, after you land the job, you need to employ different strategies to keep it, excel at it, and move up in the world.

References and Resources

LinkedIn: www.linkedin.com. Largest social network geared toward professionals on the 'net.

Job Sites: CareerBuilder, CraigsList, Monster, and others like them are the modern equivalent of the newspaper classifieds and are your baseline for searching. Search engines like Indeed.com and SimplyHired allow more refined searches by keyword. Also check with your state unemployment agency for sites that they may have set up. Here are some sites for specific job categories:

- x Sites like **theladders.com, 6figurejobs.com,** and **vault.com** focus on high-paying executive jobs.

- x **Krop.com** and **dice.com** focus on technical jobs.

- x **Careerbank.com** and **efinancialcareers.com** can be used to focus on financial positions.

- x **Usajobs.gov** is the place to go for federal job postings.

- x **Biospace.com** and **healthcareerweb.com** are geared toward healthcare professionals.

- x If you are looking for a non-corporate entry-level job, **snagajob.com** is a good place to start.

- x **Idealist.org** is a site focusing on nonprofit jobs as well as volunteer positions.

- x **Mediabistro.com** is a resource for any kind of media or writing job.

Networking Groups. Remember that only 20 percent of jobs are ever posted to the sites I just listed. It is vital to reply upon interpersonal relations and what has come to be known as the informal job market. It is best if you can rely upon people you already know, but if you can't, there are networking groups that meet up regularly so that people can help each other out. Go to **www.job-hunt.org** to find a listing of groups near you.

Career Gear: www.careergear.org. This is a program that supplies suits to under-privileged job applicants in New York City. There are other smaller programs like it throughout the country, and if you truly cannot afford a suit or appropriate apparel for an interview, you should try to find a similar program near you.

Chapter 10

PROMOTION MAGIC

As I have already mentioned, all personal finance boils down to two main piles of money: the money you have going out, and the money you have coming in. A lot of people looking to build wealth focus almost all their efforts on that first pile of money, the pile going out. People skip the Starbucks, brown bag all their lunches, spend hours a day hunting for coupons, and even make their own toothpaste and laundry detergent. All of this amounts to a lot trouble, suffering, and time consumption just to save what winds up to be not very much money. These types of measures are useful when you are in debt-crisis mode, but for long-term wealth building, they stink.

No matter how austere you are, the amount of money you can cut from expenses has a limit. On the other hand, the amount of money you can use to grow your income is limitless. There are numerous ways to do this: starting a side business, making investments, and getting promoted at work, which is what this chapter is about.

As we grow from childhood to adulthood we are constantly reminded by parents and teachers that life is not fair. Now that you are an adult you know this is true. It is doubly true at work. In a fair world promotions would be given solely based on qualifications, job performance, and, occasionally, seniority. Unfortunately, the way promotions are actually given can be a good deal more complex than that. Everything from your weight, style of dress, gender, and race to personal connections and other factors that have no direct bearing on performance can carry just as much weight as your work performance itself.

Some of these factors you can control easily: You can go out a get a new wardrobe and start showing up 15 minutes early. Others, like gender and racial bias, are not as easily combated. The bad news is that there are always going to be people who have an unfair advantage when it comes to promotion. The good news is that if you master the skills of financial sorcery, you can be one of those people! What follows is a strategy that I have employed with success in the past.

Step 1: Assess Yourself

Before you do any prayer, spell, or invocation, you need to take a good look at yourself, your qualifications, your role in the company, and, most importantly, how others perceive you.

Ask around; you might be surprised. Even though think you do everything asked of you, maybe even better than others in your department, other people may see you differently. Sometimes the person who completes work quickly and efficiently is not perceived as well as the person who stays late, comes in early, and constantly looks busy yet accomplishes comparatively little. The fact is that we rarely see ourselves the way others see us, and the way others see us is important. Find a coworker who is friendly, but not your best friend in the office. Tell him or her that you are looking to get a good picture of how you are seen by the rest of the office. If he or she answers in all positives, push them to be truthful—everyone has some trait others could complain about.

Step 2: Educate Yourself

Not everyone will need to do this, but more education never hurts. This step is all about buffing up your training and education. In the past this would mean a very serious investment of time and money, and it still may, but there are options today that did not exist just a few years ago.

MIT, for instance, has many of their classes available for free online. In spring of 2012 they will be expanding the number of classes available and offering certificates of completion. The certificates will not carry college credit, but will still look excellent on your resume and give you an easy way to learn new subjects that are relevant to your work. The Khan Academy is a Website that is providing even more direct instruction through videos on everything from calculus and banking to art history. Stanford University is also offering classes free online in their OpenCourseWare program, and provides the opportunity to interact with professors.

The thing to keep in mind is that no matter what a job description states explicitly, a job never requires a degree. It requires a set of skills and knowledge base. A degree is often just a convenient way of screening applicants. If the position you are going for states that it requires a degree that you do not possess, you may still be able to show that you have the skills and knowledge that the position requires. In cases in which you are looking for a promotion rather than a totally new job, you have a much greater opportunity to broadcast this effectively to the people in power.

My father once told me that everyone in the world is in sales, no matter what their actual job was. Networking and selling yourself can go a long way, and as I already mentioned, the world is not fair. Many people would like to unfairly give the promotion to the guy they like and feel a connection with rather than the guy that has the master's degree who acts like jerk.

That said, sometimes the paper is what matters most. Thankfully, that paper does not always have to be an advanced degree. There are intensive programs for all kinds of certificates, such as Project Management Professional (PMP) and Microsoft Certified IT Professionals (MCITP). Often these can be completed in intensive courses which take much less time than a traditional degree.

If a traditional degree is what you need, many universities now cater to adults who have other time commitments. Just make sure to do your research on accreditation, credit transferability, and general acceptance. Any college should have credits that are accepted for jobs with state agencies and are generally transferable to other colleges and universities. Remember, legitimate colleges and universities are accredited by one of the six regional accrediting agencies, not by national agencies. These six regional agencies are in turn recognized by the U.S. Department of Education and Council for Higher Education Accreditation. If the school you are applying to is instead accredited by a national agency, that is a red flag. A good rule of thumb is that if you are seeing a commercial for an online school on late-night television, your degree from there may not carry the same weight as it would from a traditional college.

In New Jersey, we have the excellent Thomas Edison State College. All classes are taught online, with rolling 12-week semesters, making it easy to earn a degree in less time and with less hassle than a traditional college. Better yet, Thomas Edison offers prior learning assessments that grant college credit for life and work experience. You may be closer to a bachelor's or master's than you think.

Step 3: Do a Macro-Enchantment

As before, choose one prayer, puja, mantra, novena, spell, angel, god, or whatever to oversee the whole arc of the operation. You make it known that you want to get promoted and what position you are seeking. It helps sometimes to make a statement not just detailing that you want the position, but also what you plan to do in said position and how you intend to use your newfound power and wealth. Some people use this to make a promise of future offerings in exchange for the promotion itself. Commissioning a statue or a donation in the name of a spirit can be a powerful incentive. Long-term commitments such as tithing a certain amount of the increased income or making regular offerings are also traditional, but unless you are very dedicated I wouldn't recommend it. Too often those deals are forgotten the first time that it becomes inconvenient to keep them. But the spirits do not forget. A promise not kept to a spirit can be catastrophic.

If your macro-enchantment involves a physical talisman, just make sure that it doesn't smell or appear overly occult. I love mojo bags, but if yours makes you smell like a potpourri store and leaks oil through your pants, it would be better to not have it at all. Similarly, that 3-inch Pentacle of Jupiter medallion from the Key of Solomon is awesome, but it will work even better under your shirt than it will hanging over your tie like you are the villain in a Hammer film from the 1960s.

Step 4: Do Your Job

Don't just do it; do it really well. Better than ever before. Be productive and, more importantly, look like you're productive. Do all the dumb things that you know you should do but that nobody ever does: Show up earlier than the boss; leave only after she is gone. Make the team and your boss look good by your actions. Speak well and make sure everything you write is properly punctuated and error free. Dress sharp and in a way that compliments your body size—it doesn't matter what your body type is, there is a way to dress that will make you look well put together, and other ways that will make you look like an idiot. You know what needs to be done. Do it.

On the magical end of things you can do whatever you need to make you projects run smoothly, but in the end you shouldn't need much magic for this step. You can either do your job or you can't. If you can't do your job well, it's time for a job change.

There is a corporate theory known as the Peter Principle, which simply states that "in a hierarchy, every employee tends to rise to his or her level of incompetence." It seems silly on the surface, but it actually makes perfect sense. Because doing your job should get you promoted, it only makes sense that you will continue to rise until you reach the job that you can no longer excel at. If you find yourself in a job that you are barely competent at, it is not time to worry about getting promoted—you will simply drown. Instead you should worry about mastering your current position or finding a new line of work.

Step 5: Get Yourself Noticed

Unfortunately it is entirely possible for you to do your job, make everyone around you look good, and still not get noticed. Thankfully we are sorcerers, and there are many techniques of influence and persuasion you can employ. As with my advice for job interviews, use magical influence judiciously. You cannot look as though you are trying to influence or it will cancel out the magic. You are trying to get some attention to your hard work, not convince the Storm Troopers that these are not the droids they're looking for. If you look at the powers of Mercury in Chapter 4, or at some of the Lightning Glyphs, you should have no problem thinking of spells and techniques that will spread your good name like wildfire. Combine this with offering ideas, volunteering for projects, and making the right network of friends, and you can quickly make a name for yourself.

One mundane technique that has worked for me is the unsolicited report. To generate this, find some metric that no one is tracking, and track it. It doesn't really matter what it is; managers love metrics, and showing that you are capable and interested in measuring what is going on in the company is a big plus. You also show that you have the initiative to do something that was not directly assigned to you (in addition to your normal duties, of course); it will help you get noticed quickly. Just make sure that your normal work is superb or this plan will backfire. Before you turn in your report, gather the business cards of your boss and your boss's boss and take them back to the temple for some late-night influencing magic. The next day hit them up with a spreadsheet of how many of their Web ads actually convert into a sale, or how much time is spent bouncing between multiple programs for a process that could be handled by one.

Whatever your individual tactics, the overall strategy is to position yourself into a spot where the company sees you as essential to their operation. Seth Godin wrote a book called Linchpin that has a simple premise: You should make yourself indispensable by doing something that no one else can do—or at least not anywhere near as well as you can. Be an artist at what you do, not just an employee. Although I disagree with some of the sentiments in Godin's book, the overall idea is a good one. Pick up Linchpin for more info on the Linchpin philosophy. You will immediately see how magic can be applied to becoming a linchpin, and also that becoming a linchpin is magic.

Step 6: Look and Act One Step Ahead

I am sure that you have all heard the advice to dress for the job that you want, not the job you have. Though cliché, it is still good advice. It may take some money that you would rather spend elsewhere, but consider it a career investment to get some proper silk ties and tailored shirts and suits. While you are at it, you also might want to invest in a style guide or employ the services of a stylish friend or acquaintance to show you how to look like a million bucks.

I for one was completely lost in this realm until a friend took me under his wing. There are all kinds of things I had not considered. For one thing, I need shirts with a 20-inch neck in order to wear the top button comfortably closed—a must for dressing one step ahead. I am big, but I'm not that big, so unless I want the rest of the shirt to look like a circus tent, I need to get it taken in to fit my waist. My neck size also means that I need a fairly long tie, and that I should use a Windsor or Shelby knot—the Four in Hand knot my dad taught me (and every-one's dad teaches them) is just too thin for my neck and head. Because of my large torso and relatively small seat, my pants should be flat-front and traditional-cut. If all that seems like more detail than you normally consider when buying clothes, you should perhaps consider getting some sartorial assistance from someone who know what they are doing.

Strangely, a lot of people have a resistance to business attire, es-pecially pagans and magicians. One of the most controversial posts I ever made on my blog was about the power of the power tie. People wrote comments insisting that only their work should matter, not their appearance. Unfortunately, because the volume of the inner life of magically oriented people is as loud as or louder than our outer lives, we sometimes get lost in ideas of how things should be rather than dealing with how they actually are. I don't care if there is no dress code at your job at all; you may think you are not being judged by how you dress, but you are.

Beyond the suit and tie, you can accessorize your business attire for sorcery without anyone knowing what you are up to. It's not good to wear a giant pentagram over your tie, but there is nothing to stop you from choosing a tie or accessory with a color scheme that corre-sponds to a particular element, planet, or god. Then it is a relatively simple matter of charging that tie—or cufflink, or scarf, or bracelet—as a talisman. I have even gotten sneaky and placed pieces of fabric with sigils inside my ties—giving new meaning to the "power tie." A friend of mine in a particularly ruthless industry has sewn protec-tion wards into his work jackets and dons them whenever he feels he needs them.

Of course it's not just about dressing for the job you want to have. It's also about talking, acting, and thinking for the job you want to have. Now is the time to stop gossiping and swearing. When you catch yourself babbling on and on, just stop—senior-level employees are more likely to be thoughtful about what they say. If you find that your thoughts at work are consumed by worrying about how long of a break you will have at lunch, how much extra work something means for you, and when your next vacation is, it will show in your actions and demeanor. Senior-level people think in terms of what is best for the department and the company and the customers. Start thinking like a shareholder. It's not about you vs. them. You are them. Use the skills you developed in meditation to cut through distraction, and cut through the "disgruntled wage slave" mindset.

The goal here is to see if you can get people to think that you have already made the step you are looking to make.

Step 7: Spend Time with People Above You

Don't be obvious about it. Start by keeping your ear to the ground. See if you can find some common ground involving a subject outside of work. Opening up a conversation about a shared hobby or even just a favorite night spot can go a long way toward opening up lines of communication. All it really takes is being in the room often enough for someone above you in the hierarchy to ask your opinion on something. If you have a solid and smart answer, you will soon find yourself consulted on things that people at your level are not usually asked about, or offered special projects that enable you to prove yourself. Eventually such a person can prove to be your champion, pulling for you when managers are discussing filling a position.

Step 8: Have a Replacement in Mind

In a shaky economy this is kind of a risky move, but in many cases unless there is someone who is able to move into your position, you cannot move up. You do not want someone who does your job better than you, just someone who can do it when you rise out of that position. Be the champion for someone to get promoted to your spot when you get promoted to someone else's.

Step 9: Divine the Timing

Timing is everything when it comes to promotion. I am not talking about planetary days and hours here, though that can be a factor. I am talking about the timing within the corporation. I am talking about it being the right time to make a pitch for your promotion.

If you can find out about someone retiring or transferring, that may be the time to bring up the possibility of promotion, or at least mention that course at MIT you completed. Even someone moving several stages above you may shake up the org chart enough to open a corner office for you. Sometimes, though, shake-ups are not what they seem at first. There are often politics and maneuvering that you don't see on the surface. This is where your divinatory skills come in. A tarot reading by itself is just a piece of data to consider, but when it corroborates a rumor you heard from a friend in HR, which in turn confirms some odd statements at the meeting last week, it becomes actionable intelligence.

Step 10: Take out Obstacles

Some of you won't like this idea. Truth be told, I would only use it in severe situations myself, but sometimes there are obstacles that have to be removed with force. Many companies are rife with nepotism or racism. Sometimes your boss is threatened by your accomplishments and works against you. Sometimes someone else who is up for the promotion plays nasty. At such times, you really only have three options:

1. Back down and accept your lot in life.
2. Escape to a new company.
3. Fight back.

I am not suggesting you perform full-blown death curses for a promotion. In fact, I am not suggesting that you do any kind of offensive magic at all. I am merely pointing out that it is traditional within the arts of magic and witchcraft, and very often effective.

For the rare occasions that I indulge in such activities I shoot for either confusion jinxes or expelling rituals. Confusion jinxes are often used for magical protection, especially when the danger is not a magical one. They confuse and befuddle your opponents to a degree that they either forget about you or their work backfires. I must stress that you should always do a divination to get an idea of what your results will be. Confusion spells are tricky and can be the cause of vehicular accidents and all kinds of more serious issues. I am not here to preach at you, only to tell you that you need to be responsible for your actions.

Confusion powder is made with poppy seeds, twitch grass, and black mustard seeds added to a powder base such as talcum. Some people color their powders, and if you want to, the appropriate color would be red. If you want to cause arguments and in-fighting as well as confusion among your enemies, add in black and red pepper. The same recipe could also be used to make an oil or incense. The clever sorceress will be able to employ all three.

A lot of people like to put confusion powder directly on their enemies or on a place their enemies would touch or walk on. This can lead to a very powerful and sustained effect, but again, unless you are very clever and careful, it is not worth getting caught. For this reason, rather than bringing the spell to the target, I like to bring the target to the spell.

It should be fairly easy to get a personal link from your target and bring it home to where you work. You can then work that charm into a packet or doll of your target and fill it with confusion-causing elements such as poppy seeds, twitch grass, and black mustard seeds. You can actually make a doll from scratch, but it takes a lot of time and effort. I usually just go to a dollar store and purchase a cheap doll that I can paint up and stuff with herbs and seeds.

After making your doll or packet, when you suspect your target is asleep, spend some time holding the packet or doll by a string and spin it dizzily over some confusion incense while speaking your wishes to it. When you are done, hang it somewhere dark by the string and let it sway.

Expelling rituals are done to get rid of someone entirely from your life. In this case from your job. Hot foot powder is traditional for this, but again, I urge care. Laying sulfurous powders down in a cubicle or powdering someone's shoes is not easily accomplished in the work space. It is better to get something of theirs and make a packet or doll, only this time with expelling herbs such as red and black pepper, sulfur, crushed hornets, and other hot or stinging material. Once you have your packet or doll, you want to get rid of it in a ceremonial fashion. Many people throw it in a river and never look back, but I have always enjoyed mailing mine anonymously to a foreign and unpleasant place like a mortuary in Kashmir or something like that.

Step 11: Ask for the Promotion

If you are going to succeed in financial sorcery you need to learn to ask for what you want. Some people are amazingly shy about this or feel that it is somehow presumptuous to ask for a raise or promotion. It is not. Asking shows confidence and assertiveness. Be humble, but be frank. Know your accomplishments and let your competence be the source of your confidence. Aim for a discussion rather than an ultimatum. Ask what you need to do to get to the next level. Present your case, and try to overcome any objections. Sell yourself. If your superiors are resistant, ask why and what they want you to do in the future. If the answer is no, unless there is some kind of nepotism or harassment afoot, be gracious. Find out why someone else was chosen instead of you, and learn from it.

References and Resources

The Rules of Work: The Unspoken Truth About Getting Ahead in Business, by Richard Templar (FT Press, February 5, 2005). Excellent guide to getting ahead at work. A lot of it is stuff that you probably already know but don't do. I read this again every time I feel like I am getting lax at work.

Zig Ziglar's Secrets of Closing the Sale, by Zig Ziglar (Berkley Trade, September 1, 1985). Make no mistake: Getting promoted is about selling yourself. Learning to sell will help you in every aspect of your professional life. This book is a great start.

Linchpin: Are You Indispensable?, by Seth Godin (Portfolio Trade; April 26, 2011). Excellent arguments for how to build a career in the new economy and become an indispensable person not just in your company, but also your industry.

Influence: The Psychology of Persuasion, by Robert Cialdini (Collins Business Essentials) (HarperBusiness; Revised edition December 26, 2006). One of the best books for applying NLP, management skills, and negotiation tactics for getting ahead in business. A classic in the field.

MIT Open CourseWare: http://ocw.mit.edu. MIT's course materials free online, now offering certificates of completion for some courses.

Khan Academy: www.khanacademy.org. Free videos on everything from international banking to advanced calculus and geology. A truly staggering free resource for self-education.

Thomas Edison State College: www.tesc.edu. New Jersey state college for adults, with classes entirely online. Solid accreditation and transferable credits.

Chapter 11

ENTREPRENEURIAL MAGIC

Owning your own business is the American Dream for a reason. To have the amount of money you can make limited only by your own ingenuity and hard work is the defining promise of capitalism. To control your time, be your own boss, and master your own destiny is a very appealing life. It can also serve as a way to circumvent some obstacles that conventional jobs present.

Do you know what Steve Jobs, Richard Branson, Duncan Bannatyne, Giorgio Armani, David Thomas, Michael Dell, and David Karp all have in common? First, they are/were all multi-millionaire entrepreneurs. Second, none of them have/had a college degree. In fact, 132 of the Forbes 400 Richest Americans have no college degree. Again, I am not against college by any means; I am just pointing out that when you work for yourself, it doesn't really matter whether you have a degree or not.

For that matter it also doesn't matter if you have recently com-mited a felony or been fired for negligence from your last 10 jobs. If you have holes in your resume, have all your experience in a dying or dead industry, or are just too old/young/ugly to get hired, none of that matters when you are working for yourself. There is no one you need to convince with a resume and cover letter. You just need to be able to actually do the thing you are doing. Do it well and be smart about your business and you will make money.

Some people like to fantasize that all rich people inherit their wealth and that there is no room for the common man to move up, but the surprising truth is the 80 percent of American millionaires are first-generation affluent—they made their way themselves.[1] If it is wealth you seek, owning your own business can be one of the keys to attain-ing it. The rewards will all be yours, but of course so will the risks.

Risky Business

Many people worry about the risk of failure and often cite a sta-tistic done by Inc. magazine and the National Business Incubator Association (NBIA) claiming that 80 percent of small businesses fail within their first five years. This stat has never been shown to be true, however, and more recent and reliable studies based on "exit rates" rather than "failure rates" show that whereas 64 percent of businesses may change ownership within five years, only 5 percent file for bank-ruptcy within that time.[2]

It is also worth noting that although a job with a paycheck might seem like a safer option than running your own business, they each have their dangers: You can always get fired or laid off from a job—something that you are not likely to do to yourself.

Starting a Business as Secondary Income

You don't need to quit your day job in order to start your own busi-ness. A good way to mitigate risk is by owning your own business and working a day job. Now that the Internet limits the need for brick-and-mortar offices and store fronts, more and more people are finding the time to keep their 40-hour-a-week job and run their own business on the side. Yes, you will have to give up some TV shows, and maybe you won't be able to go out as often as you used to, but the rewards and fulfillment of owning your own business can more than make up for it.

I am a huge believer in having multiple sources of income. There is simply too much that can go wrong with any one source: You can get sacked, your investment portfolio can get wiped out in the recession, or a business you own can go belly up. If any of these things happen to you and you have multiple sources of income, you will probably be able to weather whatever the financial storm brings. The world economy is getting tougher, and that means we need to get cleverer in how we beat it.

The different possibilities and obstacles presented by different business types make it hard to put together a linear, step-by-step strategy, so instead I am going to talk about different concepts and principles and how to weave your magic into them for success. Let's start with motivation.

Motivation

When people start their own business they are motivated by two things: passion and money. Although both of these are important, I think it is key to know which of these two is your primary motivator.

If money is your key motivator, that makes life simple: Find something profitable and do it. It could be as simple as building a Website for the local Kosher Candy shop with no Web presence and shipping their product in return for 10 to 30 percent of what they sell. It could be as complicated as an iPhone app or a new type of medical device that you invented. The point is that you don't need to be in love with what you are doing. The passion is there, but it's the passion for business itself and making money that drives you, not the passion for the product. It is pure business and there is nothing wrong with that. Given the good that money can do for yourself and others, I hope that you see how simply making money can be a great passion for people.

Although it is great, and perhaps even a better financial decision, to start a money-motivated business, experience has shown me that most of you will choose to start a business that is passion-motivated. This is where you are following a passion as a side business and making money doing something that you love. This is what I am doing even now as I write this. If you have a primary job that you don't necessarily love or even like, this is your chance to make money at a passion, and maybe even transition away from your day job eventually.

You may have already read books about starting your own business, whose primary feature is making money from your passion. Unfortunately such books rarely talk about the downside of anything. Make no mistake—there are some downsides to letting your passion drive you that I want you to take into account:

x The biggest danger you face is taking something you love as a hobby and ruining it by turning it into a career. Remember, as a hobby you do it when you want and how you want. As a business, it will not always, or even often work out that way. Do not let your business destroy your passion by making it just another crappy job. I still love what I do, but trust me, there are days when I would rather watch a movie than do a protection spell for a client.

x The next biggest danger, and the reason that many passion-based businesses fail, is letting passion blind you to the flaws of your business model. A lot of people write me looking for magical assistance with a new business. They have a great passion to do something that almost anyone would tell them is ill-advised, but no real thought as to how it will get done or how they will overcome obstacles. They read a few books telling them to follow their passion and never give up, and get a sort of "If you build it, they will come" mentality. When I ask people how they plan to overcome the obvious flaws or succeed in a business that is in decline, I cannot tell you how many people just shrug and say that they trust the gods to guide them. You may want to open an occult store with all your heart and soul, but unless you have one hell of an angle, it will fail. It's almost a guarantee. We are magical thinkers, but if an idea is bad enough, all the passion and sorcery in the world will not force it to succeed.

x The last really big danger is confusing love of product with love of the business of that product. In the last few years I have talked to a lot of people who have wanted to open occult stores. All but one of them had no knowledge or interest in sales and retail. Whether you are selling books, video games, or condition oils, no matter how much you love these things, in the end they are "units," and if you hate the idea of selling units, you will hate selling what you love as well.

Whether you choose to turn a passion into a profit or go for the money for money's sake does not matter. What matters is that you do something and make it happen.

The Idea and the Market

The biggest problem people have getting a business started is generating an idea in the first place. This is a huge advantage of being a sorcerer. When searching for an idea for a product, I first make sure that I am meditating regularly. Then I very simply perform an invocation to draw an idea to me. This can be aimed at your HGA or Agathodaemon, at a personal saint or supreme power, or at a Jupiterian or Mercurial power. In my case I most often use Manjushri, but I have used Jupiter and Tiriel as well.

Once you perform the invocation and send that call out to the universe for a good and profitable idea,[3] make sure to pay special attention to omens and signs. I also make sure that, apart from meditation,

I make time for my mind to roam freely. In meditation you are suppressing or releasing any thoughts that are not the object of the meditation; this includes inspirations and ideas that in another setting are worth exploring—thus the need for free thought time. This tends to work best when the body is engaged in a repetitive or non–attention consuming activity. Ever wonder why that great idea always hits you when you are driving to work, doing the laundry, or mowing the lawn? The body and conscious mind are distracted just enough to let the rest of the brain tap into the deeper mind and start making connections. Just be sure that you keep something like a notebook with you so that you can record your ideas when they come, otherwise they fade as quickly as a dream at dawn. I use Evernote, an app I have on my iPod, Android phone, laptop, and desktop computer at home for just this kind of thing. Whatever I record with one device, be it audio, text, or photo, is instantly synced to all the other devices.

If you really have no idea of what you might like to do, take a look at your hobbies and interests and make a list of the skills that go with them. In the course of your magical studies alone you have probably developed some research skills, crafting skills, organizing skills, and some other useful talents. See where these can be applied and monetized. What else have you done?

Another tactic is to take two or more interests and combine them. This often makes for something unique, as well as something that is marketable to a very specific group rather than the whole world, giving you a manageable population to market to. For example, a person in one of my financial magic intensives wanted to make a living as a professional astrologer, but was getting nowhere. I asked her what other interests she had, and the first thing that came up was horticulture. It is hard to distinguish yourself as an astrologer; there are just too many of them marketing to the New Age crowd for someone to be noticed without an angle. But an ad by an astrologer in a horticulture magazine would garner more attention. Astrology can be applied to almost any pursuit, but specializing helps you stand out. Spells for Investors. Yoga for Surfers. Reiki for Runners. You get the idea.

Remember, your idea does not have to be perfect. It does not have to be sublime. It just has to be marketable and profitable. You need to know specifically who you will be marketing it to.[4] This group should have four factors:

1. It should be narrowly focused so that you can market to them.
2. It should have the desire for the service or product you provide.
3. Its members should have an ability to pay.
4. Ideally, you should be a member of the target group yourself.

If any two of these four factors are missing, it's probably not a good idea.

Avoid Pre-Made Systems

There are a lot of scams and dead ends out there. Watch out for expensive classes on how social media will make you a killing, how you will become rich by self-publishing your book, or how you will use System X to sell real estate or trade stocks.

Most especially watch out for multi-level marketing companies such as Quixtar, Amway, and Shaklee. It is true that these are no longer the outright scams they were 20 years ago. Some people even manage to make a couple hundred bucks or so extra a month, but have to work their asses off every minute of every day and exploit all their friends and family to make it happen. Unfortunately, most people lose money when they get hooked up to these companies by purchasing motivational and training materials that seldom lead to increased profits.

Apart from the money and time suck, have you ever had a friend try to sell you on one of these? It's creepy. Their eyes glass over and they start repeating the script they were taught verbatim. They always refuse to mention the name of the company up front, and their pitch sounds defensive before you even get to ask them about it. Is that how you want to be? Besides, turning all your friendships and personal relationships into customer service relationships is a good way to lose all your friends. I won't even get into the silly idea of collecting money from people working for you downline. Suffice to day that there are not enough people in the world for this to happen for anyone but a lucky few at the top of the pyramid.

If it sounds too good to be true and comes to you all wrapped up in a nice, neat package, my advice is to avoid it. Schemes like that are usually designed to make someone else money!

Testing Your Idea

One of the great things about living in today's world is that unless you are opening a brick and mortar store or an Internet business that needs tens of thousands of dollars in equipment right off the bat, you can crash-test a new business for very little money. Open a Website, start a blog, pay for some Google ads, and try to actually sell your product. Asking people whether they would buy it is not enough—people will say they will buy lots of things. Ask people to actually buy it to see if it will sell. If it doesn't sell, try something else.

When I get involved in a venture I look for three factors:

1. Can I test it cheaply?
2. Does it have low overhead?
3. Will it generate enough profit to be worth my time?

Testing: When I started the Strategic Sorcery Course, I let people know I was doing it and took payment from people for a month before I wrote the first word, with the understanding that if a certain amount of people did not sign up in 30 days, I would refund their money and scrap the idea.

Overhead: To create the course, I bought a new computer. That's about it.

Profit vs. Time: The course took a lot of time to write, but once it was written, it was finished. Other than marketing, I spend hardly any time on it, yet I continue to make a profit.

Another example is from a friend of mine who invented a new type of shower curtain/product dispenser.

Testing: She made several for friends, then contacted Guthy-Renker to see if the company was interested. People there tested it and made her an offer.

Overhead: A hundred bucks or so for the materials for the first few that she made, most of which she got back by selling to friends.

Profit vs. Time: Not much per unit because now Guthy-Renker gets the largest cut, but with the amount of product the company moves, she makes a few hundred dollars a month for doing absolutely nothing.

In cases of large overhead, this ideal is not always possible. Take, for instance, the countless people I have met who want to open occult stores.

Testing: There's not really any way to test this until you actually do it. You can open a kiosk or booth at a flea market, but that is not the same and usually ends up being its own dead end.

Overhead: Enormous! If you are in a good town with many hip and interesting shops, the rent is probably through the roof. If you are not in such a town you probably would not have the traffic to support your business.

Profit vs. Time: You have to be there for it to work. Ask a proprietor of a shop if he/she thinks it is a profitable venture. It is an enormous time commitment with not a lot of payback in profit. It must be a labor of love, which is fine, but you might find you need yet another source of income. The amount of occult store owners I know who pay their bills either with a second job or from a spouse's income would shock you.

I love occult stores. I do. More than that, I love the people who run them—especially those savvy enough to do it successfully. It can be done, but it requires a lot of things to line up right. If you think that owning an occult store is your ticket to easy street, I know a few shop owners who will tell you differently! I believe in supporting occult and New Age stores however I can, but there is a reason that most of them close up within a year or two of opening.

Brick and Mortar

So far I have been talking mostly in terms of starting an Internet-based home business. The reasons for this are obvious: With a physical location you have higher overhead, a need for staff and keeping regular hours, and up-front costs that are much greater than doing a 'net-based business. It is just easier to start—and, if necessary, close down—an Internet business.

But of course not all businesses can be conducted online. If you do decide to open a store or an office, I urge you to keep a few things in mind.

1. **Location is worth paying for.** Opening up a vintage clothing store in the hip part of town will be more expensive than opening it in the 'burbs, but it will be way more profitable if people can stumble across you during a night on the town than if people have to drive an hour to some random suburban location next to a 7-11 and a pizza place. If you are going to bite the bullet and have costs, then make sure you are getting your money's worth.

2. **Do not fear local competition.** Many business owners get upset when another similar business opens in the same town or, worse, on the same street. True, some of your customers may go to the competition, but often, having more than one shop will draw more customers to both of you. When I was growing up, we used to drive an hour and a half to a little town on the

Delaware River called New Hope. Back in the day the town had three different New Age/occult stores within a few blocks of one another, as well as several readers, and a bookstore with a healthy occult section. Rather than suffering by competing with one another, the presence of so many stores made New Hope a destination for shoppers from all over the tri-state area. You would not necessarily drive an hour just to go to one shop, but you certainly would to spend the day at three or four. This is also how cities typically work: Shops of similar type cluster together, forming districts. Most cities have a jewelry district, a fashion district, and a Chinatown. New York even has a chess district of shops that sell chess boards and pieces.

3. **Bigger is not often better.** The larger your store is, the more it will cost to fill it. People avoid like the plague places that look as though they are closing up. A small shop brimming with merchandise will seem to be doing much better than a store twice its size that has empty spots on shelves. Paying for fewer square feet is also a bonus. You may have dreams of having a comfortable stage for readings or lectures at your bookstore, but you are paying for that space even when it's not in use. Better to move things around when needed.

4. **Don't think of yourself as an alternative to the Internet.** Even if you set up shop in a physical store, you need Internet marketing and presence. Too many places are scared of the Internet and do anything they can to keep people from looking at the product they sell online. I would do the opposite. Don't freak out when people start scanning the UPC label with their smart phones. Tell people to look at Amazon reviews for your product. Even if Amazon has it for a few bucks less, people will usually opt to buy what is right in front of them.

5. **Try to own the building that houses your business,** if you can swing it. Apart from the many long-term financial benefits of owning real estate, and the income from renting out any other

offices or storefronts in the building, owning your building lets you control your rent and utilities expenses. Ivo Dominguez, author of Spirit Speak and Casting Sacred Space, is not only a cunning author and sorcerer, but businessman as well. He not only owns the Bell Book & Candle shop in downtown Dover, Delaware, but also the building it is in. Owning that building has proved to be integral to the store's continued survival and profitability.

One nice thing about a brick and mortar location is that you have a lot of opportunity to work direct, long-term magic. Here are some classic examples of charged objects you can place in and around your store.

- x Lodestone in the cash drawer. Feed it every day with iron filings to magnetize the money that is placed underneath it, so that what goes out brings more in.

- x Money-drawing floor wash in the store and on the stoop. Sassafras for keeping money, cinnamon for drawing money, and licorice for sweetening relations.

- x Money-drawing lamp in the back room that gets refilled and re-lit every day.

- x Rose of Jericho in a bowl of water. This is a plant that is a big old dusty brown ball when it's dry, but when you place it in water, it unfolds and turns green. It will draw negative energy into the water, which should be changed every Friday.

- x Sigils of Jupiter and Mercury behind art on the walls.

- x Charged statues and pictures. Indian restaurants usually have a Ganesha or Lakshmi picture, or a picture of a guru that blesses the establishment. There is no reason not to have a statue of Jupiter or a picture of your favorite saint.

Funding

If you have a physical location for a storefront or an office, you will probably need more money to start yourself off than you have floating around in your bank accounts. This is also true if you have an Internet business that is very hardware intensive, like a VOIP company or a social network. Even in a home business you may run into situations in which you need outside funding to expand your operation because of a sudden increase in volume.

Perhaps you have an affluent friend or relative who can bankroll your venture, but if not, or if you just don't want to risk a good relationship by mixing it with business, you will need to know where to get money. These days, money for a small business is harder to come by than it was in the past, but it is not impossible.

First you will need to write up a solid business plan. This can be daunting, but by using resources from the Internet and some solid examples, you can put one together without too much trouble. Knowing nothing about how to put one together other than what I found on the 'net, I wrote up my first ever business plan, for a floundering hardware store to present to a large national company. That plan, along with a little magic from yours truly, managed to get a commitment of $900,000 from large corporation.

Once you have a business plan, you want to treat it more or less the way you did your resume and cover letters—enchant a master copy with whatever methods you prefer and keep it on your financial altar. That master copy will affect all copies anywhere.

After the enchanting you can apply for a Small Business Association loan from a bank that participates in SBA programs. The rules and requirements for these change fairly often so you should go to www.sba.gov for the latest information.

In addition to traditional loans you might also look for angel investors. These are individual people who invest their own money into your start-up in exchange for convertible debt or ownership equity.

A very small amount of research will turn up groups like Common Angels in Lexington, Massachusetts; New York Angels in NYC; and The Angels Forum in Palo Alto, California; but the best place to seek out angel investors is word of mouth. Again, interpersonal connections are very important in all business.

Yet another option is micro-lending, the extension of very small loans that add up to a larger sum but leave no one person on the hook for a large amount of money. Originally designed to help high-poverty areas of the developing world, microcredit is now being used by people in the first world to spur new businesses.

The 80/20 Rule

One of the qualities of the spirit of money is that money is linked to time. If you run your own business, especially one that's in addition to a day job, you will learn how vital it is to be aware of this relationship between time and money. When you are the business, it can occupy your thoughts every second of every day. When your pay is based on your sales that week, you can become obsessed with thinking about business until it overruns all other aspects of your life. Every little thing becomes a crisis that you must see to yourself.

There are ways to help mitigate this. Getting possession of your thoughts through meditation will help a great deal, as will learning to say no, and learning that occasionally you cannot please everyone. The biggest thing, though, that has helped me with time and business is knowledge of the 80/20 rule.

This rule, also known as the Pareto Principal, named for the economist who coined the phrase, states that 80 percent of result usually comes from 20 percent of effort. In sales, for instance, 80 percent of profits usually come from 20 percent of the customers. Similarly, 80 percent of the problems are also generated by 20 percent of the customers. This rule has shown to be almost a magical law that is consistent among many fields. About 80 percent of conversations use 20 percent of a language's vocabulary. About 80 percent of the plants in a garden result from 20 percent of the seeds.

This rule has proven to be one of the most important pieces of advice I have ever been given. The day I read about it, I realized that about 80 percent of my hassles as a sorcerer came from about 20 percent of my clients, and that this 20 percent almost always wanted to speak on the phone. That day I stopped taking phone calls and doing readings over the phone. I work via e-mail unless it is an emergency, in which case I charge a very high rate to meet in person. Most of my clients have had no problem with this. The few who do tend to have convoluted problems involving imaginary curses being slung at them from everyone they have ever met. They protest that it is too complicated to discuss over e-mail; I counter that if that is the case, it is also way too complicated to discuss over the phone.

As you run your business, you should always be looking for the 80/20 relationship so that you can focus your efforts on the 20 percent that gives the greatest reward and save time by dealing deftly with the 20 percent that causes the most hassle.

Getting Help

Starting your own business can be difficult. Books are not always a help because tax and incorporation rules change from state to state and year to year. If you are confused about whether to file as a Sole Proprietor, S-Corp, or an LLC,[5] or even what those terms mean, you could probably use some help.

There are a lot of places to go for business advice, but one of the best is SCORE: the Service Corps of Retired Executives. SCORE is a nonprofit organization that was started in 1964 to help small businesses and start-ups. They provide workshops, resources, and one-on-one mentoring that is either completely free or very low-cost. If you are confused about tax requirements, incorporation rules, how to manage a business, how to rescue a troubled business, or just about anything else, SCORE can help.

Other places to seek help:

x **Re-Employment Bureau:** If you are currently unemployed, your state may offer a program for people interested in starting a business through its re-employment bureau.

x **Small Business Association:** Start at the SBA.gov Website, which has a great tutorial on start-up basics, marketing, financing, and a schedule of workshops.

x **Small foundations:** These are often targeted at a certain sector based on race, gender, location, and so on. One example is the Circle of Habondia: named after the goddess of abundance, this is a microcredit lending and financial literacy circle for women based in Canada.

System D

System D is slang for what economists delicately refer to as the informal economy, what most people call the underground or black market. The term System D comes from French-speaking Africa and the Caribbean where particularly resourceful people are referred to as débrouillards. When people start businesses on their own, without registering with the government or paying taxes, they are part of l'economie de la débrouillardise, which often gets shortened to Systeme D.

When many people think of underground economy or the black market, they tend to think of highly illegal activities such as drug dealing, gun running, and fencing stolen merchandise. Those who engage in such activities are in fact part of System D, but not necessarily the bulk of it. According to the Organisation for Economic Cooperation and Development, half the world's workers are employed by System D, and by 2020 that amount will rise to two-thirds. All over the world there are unlicensed bazaars and markets that peddle everything from meat to cell phones to electrical power and utilities. Many completely legitimate companies that are registered and pay taxes here in the United States or in Europe will operate as System D in other parts of the world. Whatever it takes to get the job done is the battle cry of System D.

System D is not limited to the developing world, though. It is alive and well in your local flea market, in farmers markets, on street corners, and of course on the Internet. In fact, many companies that are now large corporations in the main economy got their start in the black market. In his book Stealth of Nations, Robert Neuwirth points out that Dick Sears got his start peddling watches on trains while working as station agent. The money he made eventually was used to found Sears, Roebuck & Co. Van Heusen shirts, which now owns Bass, Tommy Hilfiger, Calvin Klein, IZOD, and Arrow, got its start with an unlicensed pushcart in Philadelphia.

It is better and safer to run a business above board and avoid any legal troubles, but I am not going to pretend that you all will do that. System D, if taken as its own economy, would be the second largest in the world, worth more than 10 trillion dollars. The reason I mention it in this book is that you will need an extra layer of magical protection if you are engaging in System D activities—one of the Lightning Glyphs is geared specifically toward this. Whatever you are doing, I don't want to know. Just be smart and keep things aboveboard before you get large enough to be noticed.

Succeed With Sorcery

Suffice to say on the magical end there will be plenty of opportunity for both macro- and micro-enchantment. In my endeavors I have collected graveyard dirt from recently deceased town officials to use in spells that grease the wheels of local bureaucracy. I have used confusion spells on competition. I have used conversational sorcery for sales and promotions. I have planted sigils in plain sight to bring in business. I have summoned archangels and gods to save dying businesses, and on two occasions had to follow that up with magic to facilitate their sale and limit debt. The amount of issues that can arise is staggering; just apply what you have learned and meet the challenges with a combination of magical and mundane tactics.

One warning about using magic to support a side business: Keep your primary job in mind as well. If all you do is magic for the second-ary job, you eventually reach a point at which you may summon a spirit to help you increase profits, and the easiest change for them to make is to give you more time to work on your side business by get-ting you sacked from your main job!

This is not an omen, nor is it a powerful being telling you what you should do; this is you being shortsighted. If the god or goddess has never heard a word about your primary job, but hears all about your side business making condition oils, they have no frame of reference for how important that primary income is. Remember, it's not the job of a spirit, an angel, or a god to run your life. It is your job to run your life!

When to Quit the Day Job

Making the jump from having a nice secondary income stream you work on during nights and weekends is very different from making it your primary or even only source of income. You go from having the security and flush funds of multiple incomes to the sleepless nights that go along with worrying whether you will keep the house every time you have a slow week.

My suggestion is to follow the money and let the business itself guide you. Some people let their desire to escape a 9-to-5 job lead them to bank on their own business prematurely; don't let this be you. Daymond John, the CEO of FUBU clothing, worked at Red Lobster for two years while turning FUBU into the powerhouse that it is today. In an interview on the Four Hour Work Week Blog, he stated that peo-ple decide to give up their day job when "either the business is mak-ing some form of ends meet, or you feel you need to dedicate yourself to it for a certain amount of time and give yourself the last hurrah."

There are ways to mediate the impact of the jump from employee to self-employed. You can ask for part-time hours, or even find a part-time job elsewhere, basically flipping the dynamic that you had previously, when working full time for someone else and part time for yourself. You can also make sure that you have a few months of living expenses socked away in the bank in case things get rough. More than anything, though, do the math. Know what you are making and what your expenses will be. If you don't have hard numbers to work with, you are not ready.

As a sorcerer you have the mantic arts to rely upon. I strongly suggest that you consult multiple readers, and if you can, multiple types of divination. Remember, we are shooting for solid, actionable intelligence, not just a reading.

Know When to Pull the Plug

All your life you have been told to never quit, never give up, and never accept defeat. I am here to tell you that in business this can be deadly advice! As an entrepreneur you need to be able to recognize when the numbers are not adding up. It's those two piles of money again: the one coming in has to be bigger than the one going out, or you will fail.

Most successful entrepreneurs have a story or two about a business that failed. The difference between people who bounced back successfully and those who lost everything is that the savvy businessperson recognizes when something is not working and takes the steps necessary to fix it—including pulling the plug and cutting losses if that is all that can be done. We all know that the definition of insanity is doing the same thing over and over again expecting a different result. Unfortunately, that is exactly what most floundering businesspeople do: They think that if they can just hang on a little while longer, the world will turn around. Because of their belief and dedication to their dream, they invest all they have, even risking their home, to keep things running for just a few months longer, yet they never develop a new plan to deal with the underlying problems. Having been involved in a failing family business once, I feel for people in this situation. It is hard to tell family and friends that you cannot afford to keep them on as employees. It is hard to consider working for someone else when you have had the taste of the freedom that comes from working for yourself. Believe me, I know. But you must be honest with yourself and recognize failure in time to cut your losses.

Sometimes the best thing to do is throw in the towel and stop throwing good money after bad. If you are in over your head and summon Jupiter to increase your wealth, do not be surprised if the best he can do is help you cut your losses. A bad idea is a bad idea, and no amount of magic will hold it together for long.

It can be tough to abandon a dream, but sometimes that is exactly what needs to happen in order to build a bigger and better dream.

References and Resources

The Four-Hour Work Week, by Tim Ferris (Crown Archetype, December 15, 2009). This is my bible. Unlike many books, Tim gives very precise advice and workable tips for everything from geo-arbitrage to getting to work from home to automating your life. If you only get one book listed in this entire book, this is the one.

The 80/20 Principle, by Richard Koch (Crown Business, October 19, 1999). All about the Pareto Principle and how to make it work for you.

The Lean Startup: How Today's Entrepreneurs Use Continuous Innovation to Create Radically Successful Businesses, by Eric Ries (Crown Business, September 13, 2011). Brilliant rules for starting a business in the new economy.

The Stealth of Nations, by Robert Neuwirth (Pantheon, October 18, 2011). A recent and insightful study of System D and its implications for the new economy.

Small Business Association: www.sba.gov. The SBA Website is full of tutorials and resources for starting your own business and finding your market.

SCORE: www.score.org. The Service Corps of Retired Executives. Great place to go for help when you need it.

Your Office Anywhere: www.yourofficeanywhere. com. Cloud-based office solutions for small businesses.

Evernote: www.evernote.com. App for iPhone, Android, and computers for capturing and organizing absolutely everything.

Square: https://squareup.com. Tool and app that allows you to accept credit cards via your iPhone. There's a 2.75 percent charge per swipe for all cards, and next-day pay-out to your bank account. As people carry cash less and less often, you will need these. They will become useful for the salesperson on the move as well as the tarot reader at the local coffee shop.

Chapter 12

EMERGENCY MAGIC

Emergency magic is the type of money magic most people are used to. In fact, it is the only type of practical magic most people do at all; all one's energy gets devoted to everyday pursuits until something goes wrong—at which point the wands come out. In fact, there are a lot of people who claim that practical magic should only ever be used when all mundane methods fail. As you know by now, I completely and utterly disagree with that position. Strategic sorcery is best performed ahead of time and according to a plan, so that problems don't occur or at least get fixed before they get out of hand.

Another reason to avoid emergency magic is that it is much too easy to stay trapped in a crap job or living situation by fixing all the emergencies that might otherwise force you to do better for yourself. Sometimes what seems like an emergency is actually the universe opening up an opportunity that you might close with your magic. By being proactive with magic, the sorceress knows whether these little glitches might support her overall life plan.

One of the principles in Strategic Sorcery is that "emergency magic is bad magic." I wrote that to show that real sorcerers are not simply responding to emergencies or staving off problems, but are taking control of their lives and using magic to accomplish things they actively want. The truth is that no matter how strategic you are, emergencies happen, and if you are a magician, you had better use your magical skills to sort it out.

Magic used for emergencies is often some of the most powerful, immediate, and exact magic people ever do. I've often heard stories about how people were, for example, $500 short with the rent, did a spell, and got exactly $500 just in time. No more, no less. I myself used to do this kind of thing all the time in my 20s when I was living in the city. I would need some fast cash and suddenly I would get the opportunity to participate in a paid focus group, or I would find some money in the street, or perhaps someone would need an odd job done that I could do. However it manifested, it always seemed to work. Emergencies should not be the main thrust of magic, but there is no denying that magic is great at helping fix them.

Money-drawing spells are the stock and trade of money magic: You need a certain amount of money, you ask for it, it shows up. Simple. The very first spell I ever did for another person was a money-drawing spell for an exact sum. My friend challenged me to conjure him $50. So I made him a talisman and three days later he found a wallet someone left on a roller coaster with exactly $50 in it.

Here are a few spells that I rely upon when I need to pull in money.

Lightning Glyphs

You will remember that the first of Jupiter's Lightning Glyphs is a simple money-drawing sigil that can be used in a multitude of spells.

I like to draw it out in money-drawing powder and write the figure representing the amount of cash I need in the circle on the sigil. I make sure that as I draw the sigil, I draw all lines from the outside in toward the circle. I usually pray to Jupiter for seven nights and then take the powder and the written amount and carry it in a bag until I receive it.

Petitions

A petition is both a spell unto itself and a part of many other spells. Petitions can take many forms, from symbolic sigil sentences and highly detailed letters to the gods, to something as simple as your name written on top of someone else's name whom you wish to get the better of.

There are specialty inks such as Dragon's Blood that are excellent for financial magic, but if you cannot get your hands on one of these, you can also consecrate normal ink, or even a pen, to the work. Once written, the petition can be dressed with oil and passed through incense to consecrate it.

There is also an art to folding a petition. If you are drawing something to you, you should take care to fold the petition towards you. Do the reverse if the petition is meant to repel something.

There are a lot of ways to work with a petition, but the simplest is to place them on an altar and set a symbolic object on them. For short-term petitions, this is often a seven-day candle dressed with the appropriate oil. For longer-term petitions you can set a large lodestone or statue of a deity on top of it.

Money Baths

Taking a bath is a great way to reverse bad money luck or set yourself up for positive cash flow. Being completely immersed in the magic that you are trying to work seems to always do the trick for me. I have found baths to be one of the fastest-acting types of practical magic one can engage in.

The first consideration when putting together a bath ritual is the water itself. Traditionally you would use water from a natural source such as a spring, a lake, or water collected during rainstorms. If you live near a sacred spring or river, that is ideal as a source of water, but the general idea is that the more natural the source of the water, the better. That said, I will admit that most of the time I end up using tap water, and I suspect most of my clients do as well. It is far better to use tap water than not to take the bath at all!

After you are settled on the water to be used, you need to know what you are adding to the bath. Formulas typically call for three or more ingredients, usually odd numbers. These ingredients can be mineral, herbal, or zoological, and what they symbolize defines the nature of the bath.

You can purchase baths pre-made from a reputable supplier, but if you don't have access to one or just need to do it all yourself, here are a few solid formulas:

- x **Money-Drawing Bath:** Bayberry leaf, Myrrh, Irish moss
- x **Fast Luck Bath:** Cinnamon, wintergreen, and vanilla
- x **Reverse Bad Money Luck Bath:** Eucalyptus, nine pieces of Devil's Shoe String, sassafras
- x **Job-Finding Bath:** Gravel root, salt, licorice root

I should mention here that the ritual bath is not supposed to get you physically clean. You are not concerned with lathering and shampooing, only with ritual. The manner in which you wash during the bath is very important: scrub up from the feet to the head to draw things to you, down from the head to the feet to push energy away from you, and soak to alleviate symptoms. During the bath there is often the reading of a spell or prayer. The invocation of Jupiter or the four goddesses would work, as would the 23rd Psalm, or any other prayer traditionally aimed at increasing wealth.

Key Spells

There are times when the emergency is not just about needing a sum of money; it's having no idea what to do next. At times like these I use a key spell to unlock a new opportunity. I take a skeleton key and touch it to seven doors: a bank, a courthouse, a church, a store, a hospital, a business, and my home. I will also sometimes wrap cord that has been soaking in a specific condition oil such as Road Opener or Wealthy Way oil around the key.

I then take the key to a crossroads at dawn and place it in the center of the roads. I make an invocation to Papa Legba, the Vodou Loa that opens the gates, and ask that he bless the key and make it open new opportunities for me that I cannot currently see. You can call upon a different power, but I learned the spell from a Vodou priest and have an ongoing relationship with Papa, so I stick to him.

Lamp Spells

Lamps are a great way to keep constant pressure on a situation until something breaks. To make one, simply fill a bowl, coconut shell, or other receptacle with olive oil or vegetable oil. Add to this base a few drops of condition oils that impact the work, and some solid herbs that can sit in the oil. Finally, write out a petition and place the lamp on top of it, or, if you make sure that the oil does not ever get low enough to set it on fire, you can submerge it at the bottom of the bowl. Here are some different recipes for different ends.

- x **Lamp Spell to Obtain a Loan:** Crown of Success oil, alfalfa leaves, Myrrh, Frankincense, calamus, 16 allspice berries, High John the Conqueror

- x **Lamp Spell for Emergency Funds:** Fast Luck and Attraction oil, chamomile flowers, cinnamon, Irish moss, alkanet, basil, some shredded aluminum foil or metallic glitter

x **Lamp Spell for Getting Promoted:** Wealthy Way oil, High John the Conqueror root, gravel root, licorice root, calamus root, benzoin powder, buckeye nut

x **Lamp Spell for Legal Issues:** Court Case oil and Money Stay With Me oil, sassafras root, galangal root, High John root, Cascara Sagrada, oregano

The most important thing to remember about working with the lamp is to pray over it whenever you light it and to never let the oil run out. You must always refill it. Some people recommend leaving it lit all day and all night, and even go to great lengths to do this safely—for example, placing the lamp in their bathtub. As I already mentioned, I just can't bring myself to do this. I extinguish the lamp at night and relight it the next day when I can watch it. I never leave it unattended. To me it is better to keep it on an altar and relight it than it is to move it someplace like a bathtub and keep it lit. To each his own.

Conjure Hands

A Conjure Hand is also known as a mojo bag or gris-gris bag.[1] These bags are a staple of the American Hoodoo tradition and are made for a variety of purposes. They consist of the components that we listed previously, gathered into a drawstring bag of an appropriate color or bound up in cloth, as is the style in New Orleans. The number of ingredients should traditionally be an odd number; three, seven, and nine are the most common. You should avoid bags with more than 13 ingredients as these just get too complex. Here are two recipes you might find useful.

x **Job-Finding Bag:** Job-finding glyph, High John the Conqueror for mastery, gravel root for job-finding, lodestone for drawing job offers like a magnet, licorice root for influence, steady work powder, chamomile for speed, cinnamon for money, Irish moss for business x **Money-Drawing Bag:** Money-Drawing Glyph, lodestone for drawing money, seven sunflower seeds for illumination, nine pieces of Devil's Shoe String for protecting the money you get, bayberry for money drawing, 16 allspice berries for business dealings, chamomile for added power, cinqfoil for manipulation, a gator hand tied to the outside of the bag so that it can grab any money the bag attracts

Traditionally, once the bag is made you would add a few drops of oil to "feed" it once a week and to stir the powers you placed in it. Some people talk to their Conjure Hands as though they were living things, giving them up-to-the-minute instructions on what is needed.

Consecrated Jewelry

Not everything has to be done with herbs and oils. In fact, when it comes to any kind of business-related magic, I much prefer a consecrated metal talisman or paper seal hidden away, rather than a bulky bag that smells like a hippie is hiding in my pocket.

You can find an appropriate talisman from a grimoire and purchase one from an occult supplier. You can also go through the trouble of commissioning or engraving one on your own. If you have the talent, then there is power in that kind of work. If you don't have the talent though, do not listen to those who claim that all things done yourself are better than things you purchase made by others. Spending hours working on something only to have it look like crap is not adding anything to your magic. You would do much better getting one made professionally so that when you look at it, it inspires you to the work rather than reminding you of the nine hours you spent agonizing over something that you now secretly loathe.

You do not even need something with occult symbols evident upon it. In certain environments it is probably better not to have anything like that on your person. Got a golden cross or Star of David?

Perfect solar talisman! Got a silver fairy necklace? You can ask a spirit to inhabit that! Have a ring with a gemstone in it? Consecrate it to a power consistent with the stone in question. I have a platinum ring with star sapphire that used to belong to my grandfather, which has been consecrated to Jupiterian work. Take a look at what you have and work with it.

Paper Seals

If you must use occult symbols, you might consider working with parchment or paper seals. The Lightning Glyphs of Jupiter are perfect for this. Draw them out, consecrate them with oil (preferably one without a strong scent), and keep them on your person in a symbolic place. Some ideas for placement:

x **Money-Drawing, Money-Holding:** Put it in your wallet.

x **Promotion, Sweetening, Dominating:** Pin it inside your tie or under your shirt behind your tie.

x **Protection from Law, Reversing Bad Luck, Legal Matters:** Pin it on the inside of your jacket. Wear it like a shield.

x **Intelligence-Gathering, Pure Luck:** Place it on the inside of your hat so that it is on your head. If you don't wear a hat, place it inside your collar.

I should also mention that those who are used to working on the purely energetic level can install these glyphs into their subtle body in a number of ways. You can simply brand them onto your aura with visualization, or you can see them spinning and multiplying within your channels and power centers. There are even ways to permanently affix versions of them to your energy body, but that kind of work is best taught in person.

Spells to Control Speech

Sometime the emergency is not a need for money, but a need to stop someone else who is sabotaging your efforts. This happens more often than you might think. I have already covered spells to confuse or expel coworkers who are blocking promotions for you, but sometimes the fastest route is to affect their speech directly.

When I need to bind someone's speech there are two methods I use:

1. **Speech Cord.** This is a very simple piece of magic that requires nothing but a string. First cleanse the string with saltwater or whiskey to remove any previous patterning. Then take the string somewhere that you will be in earshot of the target, but not seen, such as in another cubicle at work or in another room at home. Tie a knot loosely in the string, but do not pull it tight yet. Call the target's name, and the exact moment he or she answers, pull the knot tight! Do this until there are 10 knots in the string, and then once more to seal the loop with the 11th and final knot. You will be a bit conspicuous, not to mention annoying, if you try to get all 11 knots in one day, so break it up over several days. Once you have your ladder of 11 knots you can use it as a rosary to control the person's speech. You can count the knots like beads as you chant a desire such as "Speak no ill of me." You can also take the cord and place it in jar of honey and sugar to sweeten the person's speech about you, or place it in a freezer to freeze his or her speech entirely.

2. **Tongue Spells.** If you want to kick it up a notch you can purchase a beef tongue from a butcher, cut it open, and place links to your target inside. Sew it up with black cord and wrap it up in dark cloth with Saturn symbols on it. Freeze it, sweeten it, or burn it for the desired effect upon the speech of the target. I have one student who ate the tongue after the spell and

claimed to be able to get the target to agree to whatever he asked from that point forward.

Jupiter and the Goddesses

Returning to the chapter on Jupiter and the four goddesses, if you are in need of a complete financial makeover, let me recommend the following.

Set up an altar with the Seal of Jupiter from Agrippa drawn on the altar cloth. Place one blue candle in the center that has the sigil of Jupiter etched or painted onto it as well as your own name or seal. At the four other points of the seal place four other blue or white candles that have the names of the four goddesses written upon them.

Light the center candle and perform the invocation to Jupiter. Follow this with the invocation of the four goddess attendants and light their candles when you speak their names in the invocation. After the invocation you can ask for help in your own words. Just be sure to address all the figures. Say something like this:

> Oh Father Jove, All Good and All Powerful, please rescue me from my own lack of wisdom. Guide me in the ways of financial stability. Bless my efforts with success and increase my holdings in this world. By your name I call upon Libertas to free me from the bonds of debt and servitude. I call upon Victoria to win my fights against debt and distraction. I call upon Concordia, that all may look kindly upon me and assist me in my efforts. I call upon Abundantia that I may become wealthy on both the inner and outer levels.

Follow this call for help with the mantra, IOVIS OPTIMUS MAXIMUS. Repeat it slowly and loudly, each time getting more and more forceful. You can accompany it with a drum or banging if you wish. At the last repetition add the syllable "HO!" to release the power. IOVIS OPTIMUS MAXIMUS HO!

Do this nine nights in a row during the hour of Jupiter. After the ninth night allow the candles to burn down. Even if you have to keep lighting them every night for a week, you should continue until they are burned down.

Mundane Steps

Most of this chapter has been about spell craft rather than strategy. This is appropriate because we are talking about dealing with emergency situations that affect your other strategies for job finding, promotion, or money management. Still, we must not forget that magic and mundane steps should always be taken together, and emergencies are no exception.

If you need money in a hurry, you cannot sit around and wait for your spell to work. You need to go out and create some opportunities through which that magic can manifest. It is when people do a spell for money and sit on their laurels that bad things happen. This is where the aunt dies, leaving you $10,000 in her will, or your car gets hit hard enough to generate an insurance payout in the amount of money you needed, but is still drivable. Yes, you get your money, but now you are driving a beat-up car or have a dead aunt.[2]

There are a lot of ways to get money in a hurry, but not all of them are good. Some are easy and fast but don't yield much cash. Others make you more cash but are maybe not as fast as you need. Still others may have serious financial penalties. Here are some ideas for you to work into your emergency strategies.

   x **Sell Your Stuff:** Everybody has stuff they can get rid of. You may even own something that is worth more than you think.

If you have a blog, you can start there. Amazon, eBay, and Craigslist are online options with a wide audience. I would suggest a yard sale or flea market, but more often than not, the shoppers that frequent such events are looking to spend so little that unless you happen to have a metric ton of blue glass bottles lying around the house, it just is not worth it.

x **Mystery Shopping:** Not a good way to make big bucks, and not a way to get it on demand. Still, it can be a fun way to make some spare cash, and your magic might just make the stars align to get you the right assignment at the right time.

x **Advertize on Your Vehicle:** There are companies who will pay $100 to $1,000 to you for the right to advertize their company on your vehicle. Go to GetPaidtoDriver.com and see what is available.

x **Part-Time Job:** Pretty obvious, but worth mentioning. If you can't wait two weeks for a paycheck, look into waiting tables or bartending, where you get paid in tips. It doesn't have to be a great job, just one that gives you what you need. When the emergency is over you can quit—or you can use the extra cash to start investing in your retirement.

x **Food Pantries and Emergency Assistance:** Are things really bad? Look for food pantries and other programs that offer help either from the state or from churches and charities. It is not something that pays you directly, but money not spent on food, or interview clothes, is money in your pocket.

x **Rent out Parking Space:** Do you live near a train station with a lot that gets filled up? If you have a driveway, you can rent a spot in your yard to a commuter on a monthly basis. I know someone who makes an extra $600 a month this way.

x **Medical Testing:** This can actually yield some big money depending upon what you are willing to do. I have a friend who made several thousand dollars participating in a five-day study of sleep deprivation. Most of the time it is a few hundred dollars to try a new vaccine. Look for research facilities and keep looking at their announcements for studies you qualify for.

x **Sell Yourself:** I don't mean like that! I mean your plasma, hair, and perhaps even sperm or eggs. Most hospitals will let you donate plasma twice a week. Sperm donation is more complicated and requires a commitment of at least six months of regular visits, during which you are not allowed to masturbate or have sex.

x **Turking:** Some companies are so automated that they pay people online to perform the few tasks that cannot be turned over to a machine. The name Turking comes from the 18th-century chess-playing automaton that was later revealed not to be a machine at all, but a chess master hidden inside a contraption that made it look like a machine. It does not pay much, but you can go to Amazon's Mechanical Turk Website, https://www.mturk.com/mturk/welcome, and see the thousands of Human Intelligence Tasks (HITs) that are available and what they pay.

x **Focus Groups:** I did this several times when I was younger and it was a quick way to make 50 to 100 bucks. Plus, many of them are fun!

x **Raiding Retirement:** I will talk about investments and retirement funds in the next chapter, but I would be remiss if I did not at least mention the possibility of withdrawing funds from a retirement account. This often comes at a very steep penalty unless you are past retirement age. There are options though: You can sometimes take a 60-day IRA loan. If you're buying a house, you can usually withdraw $10,000 from an IRA for a down payment without penalty. Check with your bank to see all the rules that may apply to your situation. Medical situations, unemployment status, disability—all may impact the penalty that you pay for early withdrawal. In general, though, it is almost always a bad idea to touch retirement savings. Unless someone is going to break your legs, try to find another way.

x **Raiding Life Insurance:** If you have whole life insurance you are paying extra for the ability to withdraw money from it before you die. Again, not something I would recommend, but an option in truly dire situations.

These are just a few options for emergencies; I am sure that you can think of many others. I don't recommend them as perpetual secondary income streams, but they can be great for making some quick cash in a pinch. Just remember to always meet your magical efforts with cunning efforts in the mundane world as well.

References and Resources

Encyclopedia of 5,000 Spells, by Judika Illes (HarperOne, March 31, 2009). Is 5,000 spells enough for you? Judica knows her stuff. This should be on everyone's shelf.

Craigslist: www.craigslist.org. Great place to sell your stuff and make some quick cash. Even if you think no one wants it, trust me, someone on Craigslist wants it.

eBay: www.ebay.com. Auction your stuff. Many people are able to turn eBay into a tidy secondary income for themselves, but it is also good for quick cash.

Centerwatch: www.centerwatch.com. Global resource for finding clinical trials that might pay you for participation. Also see the National Institute of Health at www.nih.gov/health/clinicaltrials/index.htm.

Amazon Mechanical Turk: www.mturk.com. Make money Turking online.

Find Focus Groups: www.findfocusgroups.com. Find paying focus groups near you.

Chapter 13

PASSIVE INCOME

Everything we have talked about so far, from killing debt to job magic to secondary income streams, leads you here. Now that you are making money, it is time to learn how to make your money make money. This is the stuff that will start to build wealth exponentially when you are younger; more importantly, it is the type of income you will need when you retire. This is the stuff that makes the difference between retiring at 65 or earlier and spending your days enjoying life, or spending your golden years as a greeter at the local Walmart.

Income you receive on a regular basis with little to no time required to maintain it is called passive income. Passive income can be made through investing and through business. Because most people will already be somewhat familiar with investing, let's start there.

Introduction to Investing

If you are an adult and you only have money in a checking account and a savings account, you are screwing up. Royally. Everyone should have money set aside to invest. If I could travel back in time to my 18-year-old self and only had 2 seconds to transmit a message that I knew he would follow, it would be to invest early.

As a child of Generation X, when I was in my 20s, I and just about everyone I knew was what was then referred to as a slacker. Being a slacker, I, like many of you, thought that my late teens and 20s were not the time to worry about such things as investing. By my early 30s I had a 401k and Roth IRA, but still had no real idea of what I was doing. Now, in my late 30s, I am kicking myself for being so stupid. Why am I stupid? Compound interest.

Compound interest is magic. It's beautiful magic. If you are in your early 20s I urge you strongly to scrape a few bucks together to invest. When I was that age I did not make a lot of money and would tell myself that I did not have enough to make a meaningful investment, yet when I wanted a guitar, a computer, a video game, or even a car, I somehow found the money. You can do the same thing with investing. Your 38-year-old self will thank you for it. Your 65-year-old self will kiss you for it.

For those who have no idea what compound interest is, the idea is simple: The interest on an investment is added back to the principal so that you earn interest on the principal and the interest earned up to that point. So if you invest $2,000 in a year in an IRA or portfolio that pays 8 percent interest (slightly below average for an index fund that follows the market), you will have $2,160 the following year. The next year you will earn interest on the $2,160. It grows exponentially every year, but you don't start getting into the jaw-dropping numbers until several years down the road—thus the need to do it early.

Let's take the example of $2,000 invested in an index fund when you are 20 years old, which is then left on its own in a fund that compounds once per year. You do not contribute anything else but that original $2,000. Let's take a look.

- x 1st year—age 21: As I said, at 8 percent interest, you wind up with $2,160.

- x 2nd year—age 22: Your $2,160 earns interest and becomes $2,332.

- x 5th year—age 25: In five years you have $2,938.66; you made $938.66 for doing nothing but leaving $2,000 to sit for five years. That is almost half of your principal. But wait, it gets better!

- x 10th year—age 30: In 10 years at age 30 you will have $4,317.85. You made $2,317.85 by letting $2,000 sit untouched. Talk about easy money.

- x 20th year—age 40: In another 10 years at age 40 you will have $9,321.31. You made more than seven grand for not doing a damn thing but leaving money to sit in an account! But wait, what if you wait the full 45 years until you retire at 65?

- x 45th year—age 65: You now have $63,840.90!

Now here is the rub. If I wait until I'm 25 to make that initial $2,000 investment, just five years later, I only retire with $43,450. That five-year wait cost you almost 20 grand! You feel stupid now, don't you? Me too.

Automate Your Savings

Of course, you won't be putting $2,000 in an account only once. Just as you have your taxes automatically taken out for you, you should go to your bank and set up an automatic withdrawal to your savings account that happens every time you get paid. Get that money out of your Mercurial checking account where the money is used for day-to-day things and into the Jupiterian palace of your online savings account, where more long-term thinking happens.

By having the bank automatically move the money every pay period, you take the human element out of the decision. Similar to your taxes, you cease to obsess over it because it is just gone.

Using the same rate as before, if we manage to invest just $2,000 a year, every year, here is what our investment looks like:

x 1st year—age 21: It's the same: you wind up with $2,160. Total investment of $2,000.

x 2nd year—age 22: Your $2,160 earns interest and becomes $4,320. Total investment of $4,000.

x 5th year—age 25: In five years you have $12,454.18. Total investment of $10,000. It's only a gain of $2,454.18. Still not that impressive, but look what happens in another five years.

x 10th year—age 30: In 10 years at age 30 you will have $30,971.33. Total investment of $20,000, but you made $10,971 in interest. Now we are getting somewhere!

x 20th year—age 40: In another 10 years at age 40 you will have $98,155.33. You have invested $40,000 but you made $58,155.33 profit. Yes, it took 20 years, but you just made $50,000 for doing nothing but putting away a relatively small amount of money.

x 45th year—age 65: You now have $830,123.12. Total investment of $90,000 from you over the course of your career gets you $740,123.12—nearly three quarters of a million dollars!

Of course, you will not be investing just $2,000 a year, because with the information from the previous chapters you will have a lot more to put away than 6 dollars a day. Go to www.moneychimp.com and play with the compound interest calculator. If that doesn't give you the motivation to invest, nothing will!

Don't get discouraged if you are not young, though. Whatever age you are, invest now. If you are 65 you can still invest! Remember, that

$2,000 a year becomes $58,000 after 20 years, and chances are you will still be kicking around at 85 years old.

How to Start

So how do you start socking money away? Well, different people have different strategies, but you start where the free money is. I consider the following two steps to be no-brainers.

1. 401k—Your 401k at your job is the first place to invest. Max it out. You are investing money before income tax and only pay taxes on what you withdraw. This is especially true if your employer does matching contributions. Why would you turn down free money? If you are not maxing it out, you are missing out on free money!

2. Roth IRA—Tax wise, Roth IRAs are even better than a 401k. You pay taxes on what you put it in but pay nothing on what you withdraw. Looking at our previous example, you would pay taxes on the initial $2,000 a year, but pay nothing on the $830,123.12 at age 65! That is huge.

Stocks and Bonds and Balance

I am not going to get into targeted investing and individual stocks here. Different people give different advice, and I do not want to get out of my depth. There are different strategies, most of which have been shown to succeed or fail at a similar rate. It is largely a matter of how comfortable you feel.

In general, as with most things in business, it is a matter of balancing risk and return. Money in stocks can return 10 to 11 percent per year, but the risk is high. Bonds are much safer but have an average return of 5.2 percent; still better than your savings account, but not by much.

Some will tell you that you should have a financial advisor or fund manager handle this for you—they are the professionals, after all. Others will point out that most of the time these advisors fail to beat the market average, and get paid for doing something that could better be accomplished with a computer program. Some will tell you to diversify heavily so that during recessions and crashes you do not get wiped out. Others will tell you that focusing on a few investments will force you to look closely at the market and make decisions that will ultimately yield more. Some people like to gather all their assets into the middle of the road, while others use a barbell strategy to hedge their bets—keeping some money in extremely high-risk targeted investments and the rest in extremely safe treasury bonds. Whatever you do is up to you. Get educated and get invested.

In the previous example I used an index fund because they reflect the market itself. Unless you are in love with the markets, choosing your own stocks is something you won't want to spend time and energy doing. Mutual funds, by contrast, are chosen by professionals, and thus have hefty fees to pay the salaries of the experts—most of whom, as I have mentioned, fail to beat the market overall. Index funds are chosen by computer to allocate assets according to the overall market. Investing in several index funds gives you a comprehensive view of the market. At the end of the night when you are listening to Money Market on NPR and they tell you the Dow and S&P did X, you have a pretty good idea of what your investment did as well. Of course, I strongly recommend not listening to such news on a daily basis for that exact reason.

As you get older your asset allocation will change because you will start accessing your investments and will need them to be much more stable than when you are younger. This is where the mix of bonds vs. stocks vs. cash comes in. When you're younger you want a higher percentage of stocks to bonds and cash because they earn higher interest and you have years ahead of you to make up any losses. The market does well overall. As you near retirement you want a higher percentage of your assets in cash and bonds because they are safer than stocks and you will need to access the money sooner rather than later. If you can't be bothered changing your asset allocation based on your current age, then invest in lifecycle funds—index funds that allocate your assets based on age. Ramit Sethi, author of I Will Teach You to Be Rich, points out that if more people had lifecycle funds, not as many retirees would have gotten wiped out during the 2008 banking crisis because the funds would have automatically allocated a lot of their assets to bonds by that point.

Investment Magic

Okay, now that we have a handle on investing, we can get down to talking about sorcery. In most cases this is a two-step strategy:

1. Divination about the funds and amount of investing you do
2. Long-term macro-enchantment aimed at the overall health of your portfolio

That is all you do. Don't screw with it outside of that. Unless you are a day trader, Forex trader, hedge fund manager, or other type of professional broker, anything more than this is overkill. If you do fall into one of these categories you fall beyond the scope of this book. I do know of a cabal of sorcerer/traders who use my multiple-divination–type intelligence-gathering strategy, which I presented in The Sorcerer's Secrets, to choose stocks. They have gotten back to me with some promising field reports, but trading is their passion. For the rest of us, it's divination and macro-enchantment—specifically, invocation.

There are a lot of beings that you can invoke to look over your investments. Certainly Jupiter and Mercury both would be appropriate, as would Habondia, Ganesha, Dzambhala, and the spirits mentioned in this book. A great friend of mine who is a successful investor uses Baphomet.

Baphomet is a much misunderstood figure who has been confused with Satan by both opponents of the occult and by some Satanists themselves. But in fact, Baphomet is something of an alchemical fig-ure representing the great work, and is also the anthropomorphic rep-resentation of life itself. The name has many possible origins, from a corruption of Mohammed traced back to the crusades, to "The Baptism of Wisdom" (Baphe Metous), which is the interpretation I prefer. The most famous representation of him was made by Eliphas Levi, showing him with a goat's head, cloven hooves, wings, breasts, a caduceus, an upright pentagram on his forehead, and a torch extend-ing from the top of his head. His arms are tattooed with the words solve and coagula, which means "dissolution" and "coagulation," indicating his alchemical nature.

It is this alchemical nature and his connection to the ebb and flow of life that makes Baphomet ideal for influencing the stock market, which is, after all, linked to the actual feelings, thoughts, and habits of billions of people all over the world.

Other Types of Passive Income

Last summer I met a friend of a friend at his beach house on Long Beach Island. We got to talking, and he told me that he was a fireman close to retiring, and had been a fireman all his life. Knowing that owning a beach property in addition to another house in New Jersey is not cheap, and that firemen are not widely known for their vast wealth, I asked him how he managed to swing it. Turns out that apart from working as a fireman he also owns a bagel shop. Note the differ-ent words: he works as a fireman; he owns a bagel shop.

His job as a fireman is like many people's jobs. He spends a full work week doing his job in exchange for a regular paycheck. He is working for his check, just as most people are. The bagel shop is an-other story. He doesn't work there. He doesn't even manage it. He owns it. Other than stopping there once a week for bagels and giv-ing any weekly instructions to the manager, as well as spending a few hours each quarter on paperwork, the money he draws from the busi-ness is not directly linked to his time in the way that a paycheck is.

Remember that one of the qualities of the spirit of money is that it is linked to time. Someone working 80 hours a week for $70,000 a year has a relative income that is far less than someone who works 40 hours a week for the same pay. In the case of our bagel shop–owning fireman, the fact that the income he gets out of the bagel shop does not require a large weekly time investment makes that money incredibly valuable.

Owning a business that you do not work at is just one type of passive-income business. There are others. Though I hesitate to divide it up firmly, passive income usually falls into one of two categories: residual income and leveraged income.

Residual Income

People define residual income differently. Some people define it as income that streams in throughout a long period of time based on work done one time. The classic example is royalties from intellectual property. Although at the moment I am working hard writing this book, once it is written and published I am done with the work. From that point on I will receive royalty checks for as long as the book sells.[1]

This type of residual income also includes money from licensing a patent, commission for an insurance agent on automatic policy renewals, sales of e-books or DVDs from your Website, and so on. Anything that you work intensely on once, and then receive money from as it is sold or used in time is residual income. There may be small amounts of work required over time, such as packaging and mailing DVDs, processing payments, sending out e-mails, and so on, but to count as passive income, this should not account for anything more than an hour or two a week, possibly less.

The other type of residual income people speak about is income that remains from an asset like a house or business property, after the expenses are paid each month. In the case of my firefighter, he could choose to rent out his beach house when he is not using it. If he hires a local management company to take care of problems for him, then it truly becomes passive income. He does very little work to keep the operation running, but whatever remains of the rent after the mortgage, utilities, insurance, and management company are paid is the residual income from the operation.

Websites and blogs that make money from pay-per-click ads would also qualify. The money made after the hosting and marketing expenses is your residual income. In the case of a blog, it is less passive because you will be writing regular content, but you were probably going to do that anyway, right?

Leveraged Income

Leveraged income is income that leverages the work of other people to create money for you. Probably the most classic example of this is a contractor who hires subcontractors to perform the actual labor for him. Another example would be in a multi-level marketing scenario in which you get a commission of the sales from people in your "downline." Profit that you make for referring sales leads for people, franchising a business, or selling a product through affiliates all would count as leveraged income.

In all these cases the strategies for magic are similar to those used for entrepreneurial work, but the magic is even more important because you will be more hands-off than you would in a regular job. Magic to drive sales. Magic to keep people that work for you honest. Magic to do viral marketing. Magic to protect your investment. There are a lot of things that you will not be overseeing yourself, and well-placed enchantments can go a long way toward making sure things run smoothly.

Of course, the thing about passive income is keeping it passive, so you don't want to get obsessive about over-enchantment. You do, however, want to take care of business, so there is nothing harmful about making sure that you are not losing money or missing out on opportunities for growth.

Retirement

If you are of the Baby Boom generation, chances are you are retiring now or are close to it. Congratulations. If you are Generation X or younger, you are probably used to jokes about how you will never get to retire because the Baby Boomers busted the system and even social security may not be there for you, much less a pension. The jokes are funny in a gallows-humor kind of way, but it's a serious issue. Just because many people you know will be working until the day they die doesn't mean that you have to as well. Think about how much you hate getting up early for work. Now imagine how much more that is going to suck when you are 80. Yeah...that is gonna suck. Let's not do that.

At the time of this writing the Social Security check for the average worker is $1,177 a month—not exactly enough to live comfortably on. Even if the program survives until you reach retirement age, chances are that it will not pay much more. Given current increases in lifespan, there is a good chance that you will be living 25 to 40 years past retirement age. Unless you happen to have a state job with a solid pension, as with so many other aspects of modern life, retirement is something you are going to have to hustle for yourself. But hustle you must.

So what do you need for retirement? If you have been reading the book, you already have most of the puzzle. Get a good job, max out your 401k, start a Roth IRA, and automatically filter money into other investments, such as index funds and maybe an annuity.[2] While you are at it, start a side business so that when you are 60 you can convert it into passive income that you manage from your condo in the Seychelles.

Magic? Well, I'll let you figure this one out on your own. Whatever spirits you invoke are going to be secondary to the willpower it will take to start putting money aside for it, but like most things, once you get started it will become its own reward.

References and Resources

I Will Teach You to Be Rich, By Ramit Sethi (Workman Publishing Company, March 23, 2009). One of the best personal finance books on the market. Geared for younger people, but it still takes you to retirement and beyond.

The Only Investment Guide You'll Ever Need, By Andrew Tobias (Mariner Books, January 5, 2011). Despite the title, it is actually more of a good start than the only book you will ever need. Still, it is a very good start.

Smart Passive Income Blog: www.smartpassiveincome.com. Great blog on developing passive income.

Moneychimp: www.moneychimp.com. Phenomenal resource on investing. Articles on everything from different funds to market volatility to the use of Fibonacci numbers in predicting stock prices. Also the place with the best interest calculators on the 'net!

PARTING WORDS

Onward, ho!

I have provided a lot of information in this book on magic and even more on finances. Whereas you certainly can act on every suggestion in the book, most of you will not. That is as it should be. The instructions of any meaningful spiritual teaching are meant to be held in harmony with time, place, and person. In the case of finances you need to do some serious soul-searching to figure out what you want in life and what you are willing to do to attain it. It is easy to say you want 10 million dollars, but quite another to say that you are going to buckle down at work and start climbing the corporate ladder during the day while working another six hours every night on your Web-based business.

The books out there that evangelize entrepreneurial life and denigrate those who work for a wage lose sight of the fact that not everyone is cut out to be a business owner. If the thought of that much responsibility, extra work, and uncertainty terrifies you, there are other ways to make money. Similarly, not everyone is made to climb the corporate ladder to management. Some people want a job that does not require a lot of thought or effort. There is something to be said for a job you leave at 5 o'clock every day and don't think about until you get in the next day. Some people value benefits and stability over money, and prefer to work in the public sector because of those values. Others value doing something that they love, like reading cards, and are willing to sacrifice both money and stability if it means doing what they love and only what they love.

The point of this book is not to turn you into a money-obsessed corporate worker or business owner. My aim in writing it was to get people in the magical and pagan community thinking seriously about their financial situation and how sorcery plays a part in it. Specifically I hope that you take away the following:

x   Money is not bad or unspiritual. You should bring it onto the path instead of treating it as something separate.

x   The gods, spirits, and angels are not there to run your life for you. If you support them, they will support you, but that does not mean that you should sit back and wait for them to tell you how to run your life. If you want something, you will need to go for it.

x   Practical sorcery is a type of life-hacking and works best when incorporated seamlessly into non-magical life-hacks.

x   If you want to change the world so that people with money use it more responsibly and for the common good, the best thing you can do is become a person with money and lead by example. What would the world look like if pagans and magicians were the 1 percent?

No matter what you take away and eventually act on, I wish you well. May the blessings of Jove be upon you and ever increase your health, wealth, and happiness.

Jason Miller,
Candlemas 2012

NOTES

Chapter 1

1. "Winning Big Can Lead to Bankruptcy," by Gerri L. Elder, from the Website www.totalbankruptcy.com.

Chapter 2

1. Fun fact: Father Karras in The Exorcist was played by actor and playwright Jason Miller.

Chapter 3

1. Those with serious mental illness should not be meditating. Meditation can have side effects that are disturbing at times,

and it has caused serious psychosis and destructive behaviors in people who were not fit for the practice.

2. The sigils are from the Lightning Flashes of Jupiter set that are given in Chapter 5.

Chapter 4

1. Note that Uranus, Neptune, and Pluto are not visible to the naked eye and thus are not part of traditional astrology or magic. Uranus was discovered in 1781, Neptune in 1846, and Pluto not until 1930!

Chapter 6

1. "PHET!" should be spoken or even yelled sharply. It is not so much spoken as it is hurled from the mouth like lightning. It is a word of power that appears not only in Tantric literature, but also in the Greek Magical Papyri.

Chapter 8

1. Numerous articles have been written about this process. See www.forbes.com/sites/johngiuffo/2011/07/13/fly-for-free-thanks-to-the-u-s-mint/ for more information. As of this writing, it is still legal, but the mint is looking to crack down.

2. See www.fourhourworkweek.com/blog/2010/05/01/credit-card-concierge/.

Chapter 9

1. She borrows the term from the Enders Game series of books by Orson Scott Card.

Chapter 11

1. Taken from the New York Times article "The Millionaire Next Door: The Surprising Secrets of American's Wealthy" by Thomas J. Stanley, PhD, and William D. Danko, PhD.

2. Entrepreneurial Marketing by Bjerke and Holtman, 2002.

3. Please do not forget to ask for it to be profitable! "Good" by itself is too vague.

4. There is a corollary to this: Some target groups are so desirable that people from other groups buy products aimed at said group in an effort to emulate that group. Facebook, for instance, was first marketed strictly to college students. Soon, non-students wanted in, followed by the over-30 crowd, all because the original target group was seen as hip enough to emulate. Now even your grandmother is on Facebook.

5. If you are starting a C-Corp you need more than what I am describing here. You need a lawyer.

Chapter 12

1. The term gris-gris means "gray-gray," and indicates that the bag has a combination of white and black magic at work in it. Of course, in strategic sorcery we don't make these distinctions, but they are historically relevant.

2. The dead person leaving you money is almost a cliché among writers on magic. Many use it as a reason not to do money magic for specific sums. In more than 20 years of practice I have seen this actually happen to someone only once, and to a relative who was terminally ill with only weeks to live anyway.

Chapter 13

1. Thanks for reading, by the way!

2. We didn't cover annuities, but an annuity is basically just an investment you make with a bank or insurance company to give you a steady payout in the future in return for your payment now. You get a steady income in retirement and the bank gets to invest your money in the meantime.

INDEX

ABOUT THE AUTHOR

Jason Miller (Inominandum) had a series of psychic experiences when he was just 5 years old, which sparked his interest in the occult. He took up the practice of both High Magic and Hoodoo Rootworking while still a teenager, learning how ceremonial and folk magic can work together and complement each other.

He has been involved with a number of orders and groups throughout the years, always seeking the quintessence of the art. He has traveled to New Orleans to study Hoodoo, Europe to study witchcraft and ceremonial magic, and Nepal to study tantra. Miller is an ordained priest in the Gallacian rite of the Old Catholic Church, a member of the Chthonic Ouranian Temple and the Sangreal Sodality, as well as an initiated Tantrika in the Nyingma and Bon lineages of Tibet.

He is the author of Protection & Reversal Magick: A Witch's Defense Manual, and The Sorcerer's Secrets: Strategies in Practical Magic. He teaches students directly through his year-long Strategic Sorcery Course.

Miller lives with his wife at the New Jersey shore, where he practices and teaches magic professionally. Visit him at www.inominandum.com.

ABOUT THE ILLUSTRATOR

Matthew Brownlee is an occultist, kung fu master, and tattoo artist located in Philadelphia, Pennsylvania. He is a member of the Chthonic Auranian Temple, and is a Tantrika in the Nyingma and Bon lineages of Tibet. He is a graduate of the Philadelphia Art Institute and works at Baker Street Tattoo in Media, Pennsylvania. Visit him at www.bakerstreettattoo.com.